ECHOES BEYOND CURTAIN

RUTH MAGDALENE T

Made with ❤ on the Notion Press Platform
www.notionpress.com

Contents

Contents

FOREWORD

It is with immense pleasure that I introduce the captivating collection, **Echoes Beyond Curtain** This anthology is a testament to the exceptional creativity and dedication of our third-semester English Literature students, who have embarked on a remarkable journey of retelling Shakespeare's timeless stories in fresh and innovative ways.

Shakespeare's legacy transcends eras and borders, his narratives continuing to resonate deeply with audiences across the globe. This book serves as a fitting tribute to his enduring artistry, offering contemporary interpretations that breathe new life into his iconic characters and themes.

Each adaptation within this collection transports readers to diverse settings, eras, and cultures, while retaining the essence of Shakespeare's original masterpieces. The authors have masterfully employed their literary talents to reimagine these classic tales, offering new perspectives and interpretations that will captivate both longstanding Shakespeare enthusiasts and those discovering his works for the first time.

The success of this endeavour is a testament to the collaborative spirit and vibrant learning environment fostered within Kristu Jayanti College. I extend my heartfelt gratitude to the faculty for their dedicated guidance and the student contributors for their exceptional talent and unwavering commitment. May this book serve as a springboard for further literary exploration and appreciation of Shakespeare's enduring legacy.

Fr. Dr. Augustine George
Principal,
Kristu Jayanti College, (Autonomous), India

PREFACE

Shakespeare is regarded as the greatest writer in the sphere of the English Language, the most pre-eminent dramatist, and also a luminary name in the world of Literature. His works have been translated into numerous languages and are also performed more often than those of any other playwrights. His works have inspired countless adaptations ranging from retellings to creative interpretations. This book is a collection of innovative adaptations of Shakespeare's works to introduce the readers to his timeless artistry and shed light on the significance of his adaptations. Written by third-semester English Literature students, it aims to showcase the diversity and richness of Shakespeare's influence, alongside exploring the themes and issues which resonate with modern audiences. Each adaptation provides instances of similar themes or plots to the original play from which it was adapted and the goal of these works is not meant to replace or compete with the great Bard's, but rather to complement and offer new insights, interpretations, and perspectives to it.

These adaptations are structured upon the Bard's original narratives, transporting you into various settings, eras, and cultures, effortlessly breathing new life into his words. Each work uniquely honours Shakespeare's literary prowess by reimagining them for contemporary audiences to cherish and connect with. This book will entertain the readers as well as inspire them to revisit and appreciate Shakespeare's work in new dimensions. As written by Shakespeare himself, "The object of art is to give life a shape", I believe that through the adaptations, it does just that, by giving life to his timeless and universal stories.

Rev. Fr. Joshy Mathew

Acknowledgements

"Gratitude is not only the greatest of virtues but the parent of all others." - Marcus Tullius Cicero

I would like to express my gratitude to Rev Fr. Dr Augustine George, Principal, Kristu Jayanti College, Bangalore. Your leadership has cultivated a culture of growth, learning, and innovation. I would like to thank all the student contributors who have shared their re-imaginings of Shakespeare's plays. Your dedication to the craft of writing has ensured the success of our project. Your willingness to share your imaginative plays has made a significant contribution to the vibrant tapestry of creativity. I am confident that your efforts will further inspire our readers to value Shakespeare's contribution to literature. Furthermore, I would like to thank each of our family members for their unwavering support throughout our writing journey. Your support, patience, and understanding have been essential to each of us during our creative process.

I would like to express sincere appreciation to the student reviewers for their hard work and dedication to this publication.

Last but not least, I'd like to thank our readers for their ongoing support and interest in our publication. We hope that this issue will provide you with new insights and perspectives on Shakespeare.

Smiti Lepcha

EDITOR

Dr Ruth Magdalene. T, is working as the Assistant Professor of English, Kristu Jayanti College, Bangalore. The passion for teaching drives her along with the motto, 'If your gift is serving others, serve them well! If you are a teacher, teach well'. Her teaching interest revolve around Green Literature, Ecocriticism, Travel literature and Digital humanities. She has published articles in renowned national and international journals. She is associated with eminent academic bodies as committee and board member. Her doctoral research on 'Elemental Ecocriticism' propagates the importance to conserve the planet. She has also organized many programmes for the betterment of the students.

Aleena Shajan is a BA English Literature student at Kristu Jayanti College, with a passion for dance, social service and literature. As a state rank holder in the national Olympiad 2019 for four subjects, she exemplifies academic excellence alongside her artistic pursuits. Currently, she is also passionately working on her own novel, pouring her creativity onto the pages with the hope of sharing her stories with the world. Alongside her artistic pursuits, Aleena finds immense joy in working with children and assisting them in their learning journey. Her aspiration is to become a special educator, specializing in helping disabled students achieve their full potential.

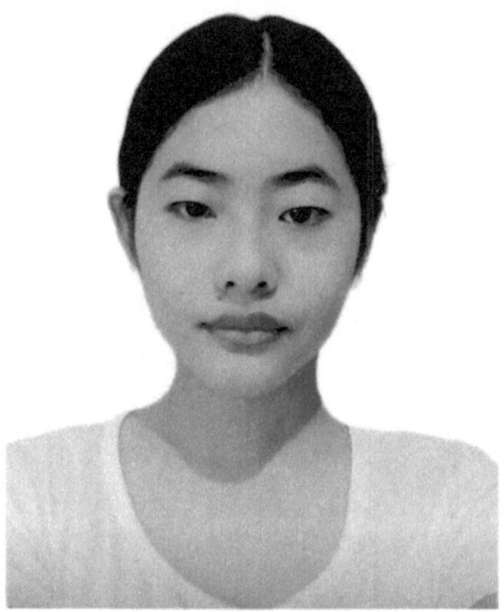

Taochirenla Longkumer, a student of BA English Literature at Kristu Jayanti College is an ardent lover of creative art, spending her time crocheting as well as cooking new recipes. With a passion for Literature and social service activities, she is the recipient of the Rajya Puraskar award in 2019 and has also secured the 'A Grade' in the open category in an International poetry writing competition conducted by AIFEST March-April 2023. She is also the Co- editor of the book 'Celebrating the Earth's Splendour' published in November 2023. Aiming to make an impact, she sees education as a platform to nurture empathy and profound comprehension of the world. Her journey is defined by purpose and fervour, driven by her belief in the transformative potential of art and learning, 'Carpe Diem'.

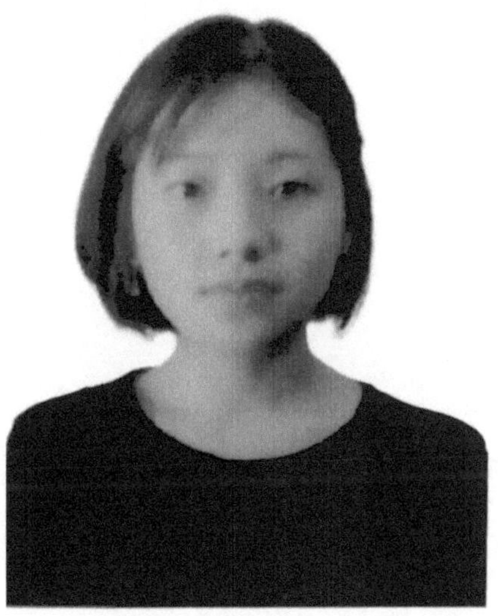

Smiti Lepcha, a second year English Literature student at Kristu Jayanti College, is deeply passionate about learning, storytelling, and personal development. She finds fulfilment in drawing and painting, using visual storytelling to connect with others. With aspirations to become a teacher, she aims to cultivate a positive and inclusive learning environment, empowering students to reach their full potential. Through literature, storytelling, and visual arts, she seeks to instil creativity and critical thinking, nurturing an environment where every individual can thrive.

INTRODUCTION

The creative and literary fervour in the lovely classrooms of Kristu Jayanti College is boundless. A group of gifted and motivated third-semester English students set out on an incredible journey of honouring William Shakespeare's timeless works, by taking on the difficult but rewarding task of transforming his classic plays into detailed, fascinating modern one-act masterpieces. In spite of all the exams, activities and assignments the students have made sure to include even the slightest of their creativity and effort for the work.

In the pages that follow, you're invited to a world where the essence of Shakespeare's genius is condensed into fleeting moments of genius, and where stories and characters are given a new lease on life. These upcoming writers have painstakingly combined the Bard's poetic language with their own modern perspectives, giving these well-known stories a fresh new lease on life.

Turn the pages of this book and get ready to travel to a place where tradition and innovation harmoniously blend the past and present. These plays offer a distinctive take on Shakespearean drama as the voices of the past and the hopes of the future collide. We warmly encourage you to join us on this literary adventure, to see the amazing skills of the English students at Kristu Jayanti College, and to discover the delightful retellings of Shakespeare's timeless classics. "Echoes Beyond Curtain" is more than just a string of words; it's an ode to the timeless value of books and the limitless imagination of young people. Welcome to a world where the past meets the present, where the spirit of Shakespeare lives on, and where the budding authors invite you to share in their literary vision.

I
THRONE OF SHADOWS - AKHANKYA SAHU

SCENE 1

(Dramatic futuristic set. Enter KING LEAR and SIR RYAN JONES)

KING LEAR: Oh, this old age is taking trolls on me, Jones. I have my daughters now to take care of our family business, not sure which one though.

SIR RYAN JONES: You know, master, what I have always told you, according to me Cordelia is the most suitable candidate. Who can pick up your responsibilities? From where you will leave.

KING LEAR: Umm... Ryan. I doubt it very much. She's the youngest and she will not be able to handle all the family assets along with the business. I think we should go for a different solution.

SIR RYAN: Master, if I have any say in this, I will suggest you wait for a while. And observe your daughters' gestures toward you. "The truest love, a compass for our hearts, guides us to the one deserving the greatest part."

KING LEAR: Indeed, It's a Good Idea.

SCENE 2

(Goneril, Regan and Cordelia enter)

(The tensions among the characters escalate as soon as King Lear enters.)

GONERIL: Father, what is it that you called all of us so suddenly?

REGAN: Yes, Father, I, and Cornwell had a meeting with Mr. Rime.

KING LEAR: My daughters, please bear it for your old father now. I have a very important thing to declare related to our business.

REGAN: *(Huffing)*Please be a fast father, we have other things to do.

KING LEAR: *(Frowning)* Behave! I had a very serious talk with Rhys. I want all of you to please me with your actions and show me your love and affection.

REGAN: Why, Cordelia, don't you have anything to say? You seem very uninterested in this whole scenario.

CORDELIA *(Clearing throat)*: Dad, I do not agree with this. We love you and we all have different ways to show that love. Instead of judging us based on this, you should test our potential, rating us on our professionalism and determination.

REGAN: Cordelia, why not? After all, he's our father, he has all the right to ask for what he wants. You just don't love him enough to show that.

GONERIL: I agree with you, Regan. And Cordelia, why must you always go against our father's decision just because you're the youngest and your father adores you the most? You always take advantage of this.

KING LEAR: Enough! Cordelia, I did not expect this from you. I let you do whatever you like throughout your life. This is the first time I asked you something and you're disrespecting me like this.

CORDELIA: Father, it's not like that. You know how much I love you, but this is rubbish. The competition to showcase our love. Love is not something to show off but a genuine act we perform towards our beloved.

(Him getting bitter about the words spoken by his daughter)

King Lear: Alright, so you don't want to prove what I ask you to?

CORDELIA: Ask. What's there to prove father-

KING LEAR: Yes or No Cordelia (his seething resentment finally reached boiling point)

CORDELIA *(Sighing)*: No, I will not agree to this

KING LEAR: Then this is it all my shares will be distributed among my elder daughters, Goneril and Regan also both of their husbands equally. I do not have anything for you in my house, you can take your things and get out of my house.

CORDELIA *(With tears and clenching jaw)*: I will move out, that's no issue for me, but rather don't take any decision just in anger, maybe you'll regret it later.

REGAN: Ha! Why will he regret throwing you out when all you did was enjoy his money and now when you need to pay back, you're throwing tantrums?

CORDELIA: Think about whatever you want and do not force me to reveal both of your ulterior motives to Father.

GONERIL: *(Panicking)* Don't drag us into this drama we have no ulterior motive unlike you we respect and love Father.

KING LEAR: Your sisters are after all right about you always crisscrossing my decisions. I want you to prove to me your potential, you're showing your disagreement with this. Leave and don't show me your face.

(Exit King Lear and Cordelia)

REGAN: Uh, that was easier than we thought it to be sister.

GONERIL *(Giggling)*: Indeed, what stupidest our youngest sister dearest is.

REGAN: We're so close to our aim sister. We are getting what we always dreamt about. After that, we don't have to keep carrying the burden of this old man's life.

GONERIL: Right, but we must be careful before all the shares are in our name.

Exeunt

SCENE 3

(Cordelia's Apartment.)

(Enter Edgar and Sir Ryan Jones)

CORDELIA: Is this the Activist you were talking about?

SIR RYAN JONES: Yes Cordelia, here Meet Edgar Gloucester.

EDGER: Nice to meet you, Ms. Cordelia. Hope I can help you with your problem.

SIR RYAN JONES: I do not know how this whole scenario turned out to be worse. I expected Master to consider you as the owner of the company but instead, he divided everything among Goneril and Regan.

CORDELIA: I know Uncle you did everything with good intentions but maybe it was my fault for not giving in to Father's wish.

SIR RYAN JONES: Now we have to alert the master about the evil intentions of his elder daughters. I heard them saying they will emerge the entire corporation once the shares are in their name.

CORDELIA: Then we must start our plan soon.

(All Exeunt)

SCENE 4

(The Lear's Corporation)

(Enter Edmund, Goneril, and Regan)

EDMUND: My spy informed, the legitimate and all mighty heir of my father dearest, that low life Edgar is helping your sister to forge alliances.

REGAN: Damnit! I thought everything would be easier with Cordelia gone, but it seems like we're in deep water.

GONERIL: Even after joining hands with you, we got no such benefit. I still don't know how to stop the protesting workers. Soon this news will reach our father's ears.

EDMUND: You two stop blaming me for your foolishness. Who told you to illegally take up the lands of local people? No, bear with it.

(Edmund Exit)

REGAN *(Groaning)*:I will kill him once he is no longer useful to us!!

GONERIL: I know sister, but not now we need his money and company support to keep our plan going.

(Enter King Lear)

KING LEAR: What am I hearing Goneril? You people threatened my employees and ill-treated the locals. May I know why?

REGAN: Oh, relax Father, we are just letting them know who their new employer is now. And it's us not you.

KING LEAR: *(glare)* What kind of absurd behaviour is this? I should have listened to Ryan when he kept on warning me about you two.

GONERIL: But now nothing can father.

KING LEAR *(scoff)*: I still have more than half of the company shares and I can kick you out of the Panel any time.

REGAN *(laugh)*: You were so blinded by your range toward your younger daughter that you didn't check what papers we were making you sign.

KING LEAR: How is this possible? Why are you doing this to me when I provided everything for you?

GONERIL: Father, you neglected us after Mother died and we need money because it's all we've been praised for.

REGAN: You never cared for us, leaving us with strangers while favouring Cordelia. We hate you for abandoning us.

KING LEAR: But- I... I thought you both wanted to stay back and play at home darlings. Cordelia was always so handy she needed someone around her all the time that's why-

GONERIL: We also needed you father

REGAN: We want to take this company to new heights, regardless of the damage it may cause.

KING LEAR: I understand you're hurt, but involving others will cause more harm. We can't just take away land and do as we please.

REGAN: We will do it anyway, and if you don't like it, leave. No one wants you here.

(Goneril and Regan Exeunt)

KING LEAR: *(Aside)* I should have paid attention to all my daughters equally. I thought Regan and Goneril were mature, but I was wrong.

(Exeunt)

SCENE 5

(The field camp, near Dover.)

(Enter, with weapons and stones, Protestants, King Lear, Cordelia & Edgar.)

KING LEAR: I apologize for my daughters' actions and assure you that I would never harm you or your family. Please give us time, and we will resolve this issue positively.

EDGAR: We will do everything we can to protect your homes and land from the bulldozers. My wife is pregnant, yet she is here fighting for you. The new owner is determined to destroy everything, but we are fighting against it.

CORDELIA: We've always been there for each other, but now my sisters own the company and want to convert this land into a dam. It's out of my control.

PROTESTANT NO. 1: We won't sit silently while they destroy our livelihood. We'll protect our family and land, even if it means sacrificing our lives.

KING LEAR: Please Calm Down-

VILLAGE HEAD: There they are! See no guilt or remorse on their faces and you want all of us to calm down.

(Enter Edmund, Goneril & Regan along with their Husbands)

EDMUND: Why my dearest big brother, I see you suffering there with your wife and unborn baby. Ops is also the father-in-law.

REGAN: So finally, the reunion of father and daughter took place.

KING LEAR: you have lost your mind in your greed for money & power. Don't you see that because of your rational action innocent people are suffering?

REGAN: Nope! I do not see anything but useless crowds wasting our time.

GONERIL: These dirty poor pricks can do nothing to us.

PROTESTANT NO. 2: Shut your mouth before we break into our range.

CORNWELL: What will you insects do huh? Beg us for your life?

(Protestant Attacked)

EDGAR: We can't control this angry crowd; love we must protect you and our baby.

KING LEAR: Son, you're right. Cordelia, sweetheart please leave the field with Edgar. I will join you soon.

CORDELIA (*Hesitantly*): But...I can't just leave you here Father please come with us.

KING LEAR: My child, I must bear the fruit of my sin. I did treat your sisters indifferently and no matter what they are still my blood I need to be here to protect them.

(Cordelia and Edgar exit)

EDMUND:*[Aside]* Why must I risk my life for these dumbasses? I should leave before some see me and try to send me to hell. Yeah, hell because of the number of crimes I've done, I think God will kick my ass out of heaven.

(Edmund exited, running)

(Two shots are heard Protestants exit.)

CORNWELL AND KING LEAR: Regan Goneril!! No

(Both rushes on)

CORNWELL *(Crying)*: Regan darling, open your eyes...

Stirring the cold and bloody body of his wife

ALBANY *(Sobbing loudly)*: Sugar bell... my Goneril wake up baby...I told you to stop this nonsense look what happened- you cannot leave me like this.

(There is the sound of the wind)

KING LEAR: *(holding Goneril, Regan's cold lifeless hand, screaming)*: What have I done lord...What have I done to my sweet daughters?

(Only the sound of grieve can be heard)

(Exeunt)

II

THE HEALING ELIXIR - ALEENA A P

SCENE 1:

(Duke Archibald's mansion lavish living room. Fine tapestries and antique furnishings fill the space. Duke Archibald sits in a chair, feeble and ill. Olivia, the gifted apothecary, stands at his side. The Duke's daughter, Isabella, paces uneasily)

DUKE ARCHIBALD: *(Weakly)* Isabella, my dear daughter, I fear the end of my days is near. This illness has severely weakened me.

ISABELLA: *(crying)* Father, please do not say such things.

DUKE ARCHIBALD: *(Firmly)* No, my child, I must. Before I leave this world, I want to see you happily married.

OLIVIA: *(Sympathetically)* Your Grace, I assure you that I will do everything in my power to grant your wish.

ISABELLA: *(Inquisitive)* Olivia, how may I assist you?

OLIVIA: *(Confidently)* I've heard of a potion, a rare elixir that's believed to make even the hardest hearts melt. If I can discover it and make it a success, maybe it may bring love into your life.

DUKE ARCHIBALD: (*Eagerly*) Olivia, do it. Find this elixir and bring Isabella happiness.

SCENE 2:

(Olivia's tidy apothecary shop, brimming with rare plants, vials, and old writings. Olivia and her trusty friend, Maria, are collaborating to make the elixir. Lorenzo, a lovely artist, walks into the shop)

LORENZO: (*Interesting*) Good morning, ladies. I'm looking for something special to inspire my paintings.

OLIVIA: (*Smiling*) Hello and welcome to our little establishment. We might have just what you're looking for.

Maria: (*Whispering to Olivia*) could he be the one?

(OLIVIA moves her hands gently as she makes a rare elixir under Lorenzo's attentive gaze)

LORENZO: Olivia, your craft is simply extraordinary.

OLIVIA: (*Mysteriously*) Lorenzo, it's not simply workmanship. It has a magical touch to it.

(LORENZO becomes even more fascinated, unaware that he is a participant in Olivia's experiment)

MARIA: (*Whispering to Olivia*) do you believe this elixir will operate as intended?

OLIVIA: (*Returning the whisper*) We'll see, my buddy. Love has a way of taking us by surprise.

(OLIVIA offers a little bottle of the elixir to Lorenzo)

OLIVIA: (*Smiles*) Take this with you. It might be the inspiration you're looking for.

(Lorenzo thanks them and exits the shop, unaware that he is carrying the elixir that will transform his fate)

MARIA: (*Interesting*) Do you think it'll work, Olivia?

OLIVIA: (*Mysteriously*) Love, Maria, is a strange elixir in and of itself. Let us hope that it points us in the correct way.

(The scenario concludes with Olivia and Maria exchanging a knowing gaze, recognising that they've begun the process of bringing love into their lives)

SCENE 3:

(A moonlit garden with flowering plants and twisting walkways. Isabella poses at a fountain in a masked outfit. Sebastian, a dedicated musician, walks in, clutching a lute)

SEBASTIAN: (*Charming*) Fair woman, may I serenade you with a song beneath this enchanted moonlight?

ISABELLA: (*giggling*) Sir, a serenade? How could I possibly refuse?

(Sebastian starts playing a sweet melody, and his impassioned singing fills the yard. Isabella pays close attention, her heart captured by the music)

SEBASTIAN: (*singing*)

"In this garden where love takes flight, underneath the stars so bright,

I find in you a radiant grace,

A smile that lights this sacred place."

(As Sebastian concludes his song, Isabella's eyes glitter. Under the moonlight, they share a moment of stillness)

ISABELLA: (*Interesting*) Sir, your music reaches my soul. But who is hiding behind that mask?

SEBASTIAN: (*jokingly*) Ah, that's a secret I can't tell you, fair woman. But I vow that when the time comes, it will be revealed.

(Throughout the night, the two continue to converse and share tales, their bond becoming deeper with each word)

ISABELLA: (*Smiling*) Even in our anonymity, I feel a deep connection with you.

SEBASTIAN: (*With gratitude*) So do I, lovely woman. Let us appreciate this moment, for it may be the beginning of something beautiful.

(TheScene concludes with Isabella and Sebastian having a hidden link, unaware that the elixir's charm is growing their love for one another)

SCENE 4:

(Duke Archibald's mansion's magnificent drawing room. The room is lavishly decorated with large artwork and luxury furnishings. Duke Archibald is present, as are Olivia, Maria, Lorenzo, Isabella, and Sebastian)

DUKE ARCHIBALD: (*Joyfully*) My lovely Isabella, it appears that love has finally entered our life. Sebastian, you have given so much joy to my daughter's heart.

ISABELLA: (*Blushing*) Father, I'm overjoyed.

OLIVIA: (*nervously*) Your Grace, I must confess something.

DUKE ARCHIBALD: (*Interesting*) What is it, Olivia?

OLIVIA: (*With pause*) I had a hand in this, Your Grace. I utilized an elixir to strengthen love relationships.

DUKE ARCHIBALD: (*Surprised*) An elixir? What exactly do you mean?

MARIA: (*Whispering to Olivia*) We should have told him sooner.

OLIVIA: (*Returning the whisper*) It wasn't the proper moment until now.

SEBASTIAN: (*Perplexed*) What elixir are you referring to?

LORENZO: (*Perplexed*) And why was that vial handed to me earlier?

OLIVIA: (*Apologetically*) I really apologize to everyone. It seemed like the only option to grant the Duke's dream for Isabella to find love. I concocted a concoction to make you all fall in love.

ISABELLA: (*astonished*) You mean our feelings for each other weren't really genuine?

OLIVIA: (*With regret*) I'm afraid not. But please understand that my objective was always to make you happy.

DUKE ARCHIBALD: (*Thoughtfully*) Olivia, love cannot be forced, but it can be nourished. I may not have known the truth, but the love between Isabella and Sebastian is genuine. And I am glad for that.

ISABELLA: (*To Sebastian*) Sebastian, no matter how our feelings originated, my love for you is genuine.

SEBASTIAN: (*Smiles*) And mine, Isabella.

(Despite the discovery of the elixir, the Duke, Isabella, Sebastian, Lorenzo, Olivia, and Maria are filled with warmth and forgiveness as they come to grips with the unique circumstances that brought them together)

SCENE 5:

(Duke Archibald's mansion magnificently designed garden. The mood is joyous, with bright flowers, music, and laughter. Isabella and Sebastian are suited up for their wedding, and they are surrounded by family and friends. Olivia and Maria are standing close)

DUKE ARCHIBALD: (*Raises a glass*) To Isabella and Sebastian, may your love grow unhindered by elixirs or secrets.

GUESTS: (*Raises their glasses*) To Isabella and Sebastian!

(As they clink glasses, Isabella and Sebastian exchange passionate glances)

ISABELLA: (*Whispering to Sebastian*) It doesn't matter how our love began; it's true now, and that's all that matters.

SEBASTIAN: (*Returning the whisper*) Yes, my darling.

(They cement their love for one other with a passionate kiss)

OLIVIA: (*To Maria*) Love, even in the most unexpected situations, has a way of finding its way.

MARIA: (*Nods*) Yes, Olivia. And it has undoubtedly made its way into our lives.

(OLIVIA and Maria exchange a warm glance, implying their personal bond)

LORENZO: (*approaching Olivia*) My beloved Olivia, your elixir may have begun this voyage, but it will be carried on by our hearts.

OLIVIA: (*Smiling*) Lorenzo, you are a wise guy.

(The newlyweds, Isabella and Sebastian, are celebrating their love with family and friends, and the atmosphere is full with laughter, music, and dancing. The drama concludes on a happy note, with the notion that love, in all of its forms, has its own charm)

(Exeunt)

III
TRUST NO MORE - ASMITA MAJUMDER

SCENE 1

(Enters Proteus and the Guard)

THE GUARD: Sir, what are we supposed to do with Sylvia?

PROTEUS: What do you mean? The only way out right now is to follow her. There is no way I'm letting her run away.

THE GUARD: Sir Proteus, I tried my best to stop her from getting away. I'm utterly ashamed of myself for failing to do so.

PROTEUS: I forgive you. I do not understand why that woman always tries to run away. I have always provided her with my love and affection. I adore her so much, but she responded with betrayal. I'm so disheartened and heartbroken.

THE GUARD: I'm so sorry Sir.

(Enters the Duke)

DUKE: Proteus, I have got some news for you.

PROTEUS: I hope it is related to the disappearance of Sylvia.

DUKE: I heard she has fled to the forest where Valentine is supposed to be hiding for a while.

PROTEUS: What? That woman is unbelievable. I gave her so much love and she still chose Valentine!! What did I lack? My admiration for her was so extreme but she turned blind and never tried to look at me. My heart is wrenched. It feels so numb. My emotions are a mixture of anger and hatred for that woman.

THE GUARD: We need to find her, Sir.

PROTEUS: Get the horses. We are leaving right now. I'm not letting that woman away.

(Proteus, the Guard and Duke exit)

SCENE 2

(Enters Sylvia, First outlaw and Second Outlaw)

FIRST OUTLAW: Finally!! Now calm down. We need to take you to Sir.

SYLVIA: Get your filthy hands away from me. All of you are losers. Leave me alone! Let me go!

SECOND OUTLAW: Now now, Miss. We are trying to be patient with you. Behave well so that Sir Proteus isn't disappointed.

(Enters Proteus)

PROTEUS: Ah! Look who it is. The woman who betrayed me and still has no shame.

SYLVIA: Stop speaking gibberish Proteus. I did not betray you. You betrayed your friend and decided to take up his position whilst he's taking shelter in a forest. How could you ever do that?

PROTEUS: Oh, enough Sylvia! I did what I had to do. I chose to be with the woman I love but you? You ended up choosing Valentine over me. My emotions towards you are just hatred and disgust. Now come with me. (*Grabs Sylvia by the arm*)

SYLVIA: Leave me alone! I should have never listened to your words. You are nothing but a manipulator.

PROTEUS: How dare you speak to such a woman!!!!

(Proteus moves in to harass Sylvia, her cries reach Valentine which worries him)

SYLVIA: Get away from me! What are you trying to do Proteus? Leave me!! Someone please help.

PROTEUS: You have spoken enough. This is what you deserve.

(Sylvia tries to free herself from Proteus but ends up hitting her head on a huge rock which causes her death instantly)

SCENE 3

(Enters Valentine)

VALENTINE:Oh my God! What have you done Proteus? Please tell me this is not true. Please tell me that she's alive, my love is alive. (*Falls on the ground near Sylvia's body and breaks down*)

PROTEUS: Stop crying those crocodile tears Valentine. She deserved it. She was nothing but a shameless woman who did not know how to repay my love.

(Valentine moves forward to attack Proteus but is stopped by the outlaws)

VALENTINE: Leave me!! Can you not see what he's done? He has killed the daughter of the Duke.

FIRST OUTLAW: I'm sorry Sir, but I abide by the rules laid by Sir Proteus.

VALENTINE: Have you lost your mind? What rules are you even talking about? You are choosing Proteus over the Duke's daughter.

PROTEUS: Well, don't worry Valentine. They will always choose me unlike that woman.

(Enters the Duke)

DUKE: What am I seeing here? My daughter! Oh my love! What has happened to you? Please don't leave me. Whoever has done this sin will have to pay for it.

PROTEUS: Your Majesty, it was Valentine who committed this sin.

VALENTINE: WHAT?? I would never do so. I loved her to the moon and back. She was everything to me. I would never think about committing such a crime.

PROTEUS: Oh, stop lying Valentine. We all saw you committing this crime. Do not try to run away from your sin. For you won't be forgiven. Your Majesty, please do something about this. He killed the love of my life.

VALENTINE: Do not listen to him, Your Majesty. He is a liar, a betrayer and a shameless murderer.

DUKE: I do not want you to speak anymore Valentine. I should have put you behind bars back then. But no! I showed sympathy towards you, and you took my daughter away from me. Outlaws, capture him and put him behind the bars.

VALENTINE: Sir, please listen to me. I did not commit the crime. Please do not listen to Proteus. He is trying to persuade you.

DUKE: Enough!! No more words, Valentine. My hatred for you increase every time you speak.

(The outlaws capture Valentine and put him behind the bars. He is framed for being the murderer of Sylvia)

(Exeunt)

IV
CASSIDY'S CONVERGENCE - BETTINA THOMAS

SCENE 1

(The bustling hallway of Xavier's High School. Students are chatting, rushing to classes, and posting flyers for various clubs. Julian Thompson, the enthusiastic student body president, stands on a platform, addressing a group of enthusiastic students. Some students are holding signs with messages of support for Julian.)

JULIAN:(*with passion*) Fellow students, today marks a new beginning for our school! With your support, we can transform Xavier's into a place of unity and excellence. Together, we'll rise above the challenges!

STUDENTS:(*cheering*) Julian! Julian!

(As Julian continues his speech, some students exchange concerned glances. The SCENE shifts to a quiet corner of the school courtyard. Cassidy and Bailey sit on a bench, engrossed in a discussion.)

CASSIDY:(*concerned*) Bailey, have you noticed how Julian's been getting more power-hungry lately? I'm afraid he'll change the school for the worse.

BAILEY:(*thoughtful*) I've seen it too, Cassy. But is challenging him the right move? We don't want to create more division.

CASSIDY:*(determined)* we don't have to challenge him directly, but we can't ignore our concerns either. We need to find a way to express them constructively.

(Scene fades out)

SCENE 2

(A tucked away area where Cassidy and Bailey gather a group of diverse students.)

CASSIDY:*(passionate)* we can't let Julian's unchecked authority hurt our school's unity. We need to stand up for what's right.

CASEY:*(doubtful)* but what if Julian's ideas do make the school better? We'll just be seen as troublemakers.

DEVIN:*(supportive)* we can express our concerns without attacking him. Let's be the voice of reason, and ensure everyone's voices are heard.

(Alex Anthony, Julian's friend, overhears their conversation. Alex stands before a crowd in the school courtyard, rallying support for Julian's plans. Students on both sides are gathered, holding signs in support of Julian or with questions about his ideas.)

ALEX:*(enthusiastic)* Friends, Julian is our leader for a reason. His vision will elevate our school to new heights! Let's back him up!

(Students passionately engage in discussions and debates, displaying their divided opinions.)

SCENE 3

(Cassidy, Bailey, Casey, and Devin sit around a table, planning their approach.)

CASSIDY:(*determined*) During Julian's speech tomorrow, we'll raise concerns about the unintended consequences of his plans.

BAILEY:(*nodding*) we need to approach this calmly and logically. Our goal is to foster dialogue, not ignite a war.

DEVIN:(*hopeful*) we can make a difference if we handle this wisely.

(Cut to the next day, where students gather in the courtyard for Julian's speech. Julian takes the stage to present his transformative ideas.)

JULIAN:(*inspiring*) Xavier's High School, our potential is limitless! With teamwork and determination, we'll achieve greatness together!

(Cassidy and her group step forward, holding placards with thought-provoking questions.)

CASSIDY:(*calmly*) Julian, we applaud your enthusiasm. But have you considered the impact on students who might feel left out?

BAILEY:(*gentle*) your ideas are commendable, Julian, but how can we ensure that everyone's voice is heard?

SCENE 4

(Bailey steps forward to deliver an emotional speech)

BAILEY:(*passionate*) Friends, we're all here because we love our school. Let's remember that unity is our strength. Let's question with respect, not divide with anger.

(The student body is divided in their reactions, with some nodding in agreement and others expressing frustration. Cassidy and Bailey sit at a table, reflecting on the growing division in the school.)

CASSIDY: (*worried*) Bailey, our intentions were good, but we've stirred up more trouble than we intended.

BAILEY:*(resolute)* we can't turn back now. We need to find a way to bridge the gap and bring everyone together again.

(Scene transitions to the school courtyard)

(Cassidy and Bailey approach Julian in the courtyard)

CASSIDY:*(earnestly)* Julian, we may not agree on everything, but we share a common goal: a better school. Let's find a way to work together.

JULIAN:*(reflective)* you're right. I got carried away. Let's focus on what truly matters – the well-being of our school.

(Cut to a month later. A school-wide assembly is held, and Cassidy, Bailey, and Julian address the student body)

CASSIDY:*(appealingly)* our school's strength lies in our diversity. Let's value differing perspectives and work together.

JULIAN:*(humble)* I've learned that leadership is about listening as much as it is about leading. Our unity will be our legacy.

(The play concludes with students reflecting on the lessons they've learned and striving for a harmonious school environment. Themes of power, ambition, and the importance of unity resonate as they work together to shape a better future for their school.)

V

THE REDEMPTION OF THE JEW - BLESSON VARGHESE

SCENE 1

(A Market in Venice. Enter Antonio Bassanio and Lorenzo)

BASSANIO: That's the gist of it

ANTONIO: And you need how much?

BASSANIO: Three thousand ducats

ANTONIO: So, you say that you wish to borrow three thousand ducats from me since you want to marry the fair Portia who resides in Belmont

LORENZO: Isn't this the very same Portia for whom thousands of suitors from all over the world have come to marry but have failed

BASSANIO: Yes, my friend. It is the one you speak of whom I wish to marry

LORENZO: So, you wish to try your luck?

BASSANIO: Not luck my friend. Something tells me I will surely win her hand.

LORENZO: May your confidence help you win

BASSANIO: It will. But for that to happen Dear Antonio here should lend me the three thousand ducats which I require to travel to Belmont

ANTONIO: (*Ponders for a while*) My friend. My heart wishes to help you but my necessities hold me back. Do not be mistaken I have no doubt but am sure you will win the hand of the fair Portia. But you know that I am a merchant and make my money with trade. However, times are tough for me as I have lost all contact with the ships that were carrying my important goods which has led me to suffer losses. So I am currently in no position to provide you with the three thousand which you require

LORENZO: Oh! Antonio My dear friend I pray that your toughness may soon be a thing of the past. But now what will happen to poor Bassanio who wishes to marry the fair Portia

ANTONIO: Not a problem. I won't allow such a minor inconvenience to pose an issue to my dear friend Bassanio. I will go at once to my merchant friends and find someone who could lend me the three thousand ducats

LORENZO: Yes, with haste

BASSANIO: May lady luck guide you, my dear friend

(Antonio exits)

LORENZO: A fine man

BASSANIO: A fine man indeed. I can't count the number of times he has helped me. The number of times he has lent me money and never asked it back. Even now he helps without any hesitation.

LORENZO: Hold on to him Dear Bassanio. Hold on to him as Neptune holds on to his waves

BASSANIO: That I shall do

LORENZO: So, this woman you speak of

BASSANIO: Portia of Belmont?

LORENZO: Yes, tell me. Have you seen her before?

BASSANIO: Yes. And whatever they tell about her is true. She is as beautiful as the Greek Goddess Aphrodite herself. Suitors from all over the world come to win her hand but fail as they fail the task which was decided by her father

LORENZO: A task?

BASSANIO: Yes, a task. No one knows what it is and all the suitors who have taken the task have taken an oath that they shall never say about the task to others.

LORENZO: And you believe you will win this task?

BASSANIO: Of that I am sure

(Sounds of footsteps approaching)

LORENZO: Halt! Who goes there?

(Shylock and Jessica enter)

BASSANIO: As if my day wasn't bad enough. Why isn't it the lowly Shylock?

LORENZO:*(Aside)* Along with the lovely Jessica

SHYLOCK:*(Scowling)* Speak for yourself you mongrel. Where is the dog who is usually at your heels?

BASSANIO: *(Stepping forward)* Don't you dare call my friend that you......

JESSICA:*(Stepping in)* Forgive my father Master Bassanio he isn't in his finest mood today.

BASSANIO: Forgive me, Lady, Jessica for my rude behaviour

SHYLOCK: Stay out of it Jessica

LORENZO: Yes, please stay out of it lovely Jessica. Don't tarnish yourself as you are the only good thing that has come from Shylock

JESSICA:*(Blushes)* Good morning to you Lord Lorenzo

SHYLOCK: No need to talk to these lowly Christians Jessica. Take these bags and head for home,

JESSICA: Yes Father

(Jessica exits)

SHYLOCK: So which one of you idiot's wishes to marry Portia

BASSANIO: How did you....

SHYLOCK: Know? This is Venice. News travels fast here, especially when it is the dreams of a fool

BASSANIO: It's not a dream

SHYLOCK:*(Laughing)* We shall see

(Enter Antonio panting)

BASSANIO: My friend

LORENZO: Any luck?

ANTONIO: Forgive me, my friend. I could not bring you the money. None of my friends hold that amount of money right now or most of them are out of Venice. I am sorry that I could not bring you the money you wish for

SHYLOCK: What is this money you speak of?

BASSANIO: Nothing that concerns you

ANTONIO: No wait. *(To Shylock)* Shylock you and I have never been on good terms. You hate me and it is not a secret that I hate you too. However, I need your help. My friend here needs three thousand ducats as soon as possible and you are the last person I can turn to. So, name your price and it shall be yours

SHYLOCK:*(Ponders for a while)* Fine I shall help

BASSANIO: Really!!!

LORENZO: A Jew helping a Christian. And people say that there are no miracles

ANTONIO: And your price?

SHYLOCK: A pound of your flesh

BASSANIO: What!!!

SHYLOCK: Yes, if you fail to pay me the money back with interest in a month's time you shall have to pay me with a pound of your flesh

BASSANIO: Dear Antonio, you shall do no such thing for me. I would rather throw away my dream of marrying Portia than see you hurt yourself

ANTONIO: Don't worry my friend. I am sure I can pay this monster back the amount before the month ends as I am sure my ships will arrive by that time and then I will make sure to come to your wedding. (To Shylock) Move on Shylock and let's write the bond despite how ridiculous it may sound.

SHYLOCK: Excellent!!!

LORENZO: Oh, You Monster. May you suffer a thousand times over for this.

SHYLOCK: Silence you cur!!!

ANTONIO: Calm down Lorenzo. Lead the way Shylock, and I shall follow

(Shylock exits)

ANTONIO:(*Hugging Bassanio*) I will send the money as soon as I get it. However, I won't be able to bid you farewell when you leave for Belmont

BASSANIO: Don't worry my friend I will win the hand of the beautiful Portia and return as soon as possible.

(*Exit*)

SCENE 2

(A Castle in Belmont. Enter Portia and Nerissa)

PORTIA: What you say is true?

NERISSA: Yes, my lady. Our messengers have told us that Bassanio from Venice will be coming to Belmont to try his luck with marriage

PORTIA: Isn't it the same Bassanio?

NERISSA: Yes, My lady. The one whom you had seen before and had been enchanted with

PORTIA: My dear Nerissa. If my late father's wishes would not have binded me, I would have married the man my heart seeks. What a sad life I lead. To not be able to reject the man I dislike and not to accept the proposal of the man I like

NERISSA: My Dear Lady. What you say is indeed woeful. However, your father was a great man and I am sure that the task he has chosen, which is to choose the correct casket will give you the husband who will be right for you

PORTIA: And what if the husband who is right for me not be the one, I desire

NERISSA: I pray that such a situation does not take place

(Sound of trumpets and celebrations)

NERISSA: Sounds like he has arrived

PORTIA: Let's go with haste Nerissa and meet the man who might become my husband or one of the suitors who tried to win me

(Exit Portia and Nerissa)

(A Garden in Venice. Enter Lorenzo and Jessica)

JESSICA: And how long will it take

LORENZO: Soon my love

JESSICA: My Dear Lorenzo. Do it by tonight. The hate of my father for you Christians increases day by day. The possibility of him accepting our love decreases day by day.

LORENZO: Then tell me what should I do, love?

JESSICA: Take me out of that hell. Take me out of there before I forget what being loved feels like. My home feels like a jail were my father always curses the Christians

LORENZO: Tonight, my love. In the cover of the night Gratanio and I will pick you up from your father's house and take you away with me.

JESSICA:(*Holding hands*) That sounds wonderful.

(Exeunt. A room in Portia's castle)

PORTIA: Here lies Lord Bassanio, the three caskets that will decide my fate. Whether I will be your wife or not

BASSANIO: There are three caskets, my lady. A gold, a silver and a lead. How shall I know I have picked the right casket?

PORTIA: One of these contains a portrait of mine. If you pick the casket that has my portrait in it. You can have me in body and soul

BASSANIO: The gold one is beautiful. It is like an illusion. The tombs which are made of gold appear beautiful but have nothing but dead bodies inside. The silver one on the other hand is common. Something as precious as Portia cannot be in you. However, you lead. You are common and unappreciated but have many uses. The portrait of someone as great as Portia can only be in someone as great as you.

(Opens the lead casket and finds the portrait inside)

PORTIA: My Lord nothing in this entire world can describe my happiness which I am feeling at this moment. I belong to you in mind, body and soul. Accept me as your wife along with everything I have. For I am yours and you are mine.

NERISSA: Congratulations my Lord and Lady. May the wheels of love and fortune forever drive your life.

(A messenger arrives and hands a letter to Bassanio)

PORTIA: What's the matter my love? I can feel your face turning to that of despair

BASSANIO: It is my friend, my lady. A friend who is thought of as a brother. Who borrowed three thousand ducats from an evil Jew money lender to help me come here? His ships have been destroyed and he is in no way able to pay the money back. And now the moneylender goes after his life. I must return immediately to help him out

PORTIA: With haste my love. Nerissa hand him the three thousand ducats in order to pay the merchant off. Save this friend of yours my love for a great man such as this should not be killed.

(Exeunt)

SCENE 3

(Outside Shylock's house at night)

LORENZO: My Love I am here.

GRATIANO: Are you sure this is the house

LORENZO: As sure as I can be

GRATIANO: And you could not love anyone else other than the Jew's daughter.

LORENZO: The Jew's daughter is nothing like her father. She is an angel compared to him and I know that.

GRATIANO: If you say so

(Enter Jessica from the top of the building)

LORENZO: My love. Don't seek from the top for I have come to get you away from her

(Jessica throws down a rope)

JESSICA: Climb up my love for I have something for you

(Lorenzo climbs up with the help of a rope)

LORENZO: What is it, my love?

(Jessica brings up a heavy bag and gives it to Lorenzo)

LORENZO: What's in this my love?

JESSICA: Gold and ornaments from my father's treasury

LORENZO: But why are you giving it to me my love?

JESSICA: We can use this to live a happy life. I don't think my father has any use for this. He is already old. He will have no use of this much gold and money.

LORENZO: I can't.

JESSICA: What?

LORENZO: I can't love.

JESSICA: Why do you say no?

LORENZO: Yes, I hate your father because he is a Jew and right now, I am taking his daughter from him. I can't take his money from him as well. I can't do that to the old man

JESSICA: I did not think like that.....

LORENZO: I know. I don't need these riches either way. We are going to Belmont where Bassanio has won the hand of Lady Portia.

JESSICA: That's fantastic news you bring my friend

(A series of footsteps is heard. A servant enters)

SERVANT: Lady Jessica Lord Shylock is rushing to the house. One of the servants told him of your plot and he is rushing towards the mansion. Kindly hurry!

JESSICA: My Love let's run away as far as we can.

LORENZO: Yes, let's do that my love.

(Jessica and Lorenzo exit. Shylock enters)

SHYLOCK: Jessica! Jessica! Where is that ungrateful wretch?

SERVANT: My Lord she eloped with the Christian Lorenzo.

SHYLOCK: My gold and ornaments. The wretch took it all. I have nothing left for my name. My daughter elopes with a Christian and I have lost all my possessions

SERVANT: No, my lord. Your gold is right here. Lady Jessica wanted to take away this too but Lord Lorenzo talked her out of it.

SHYLOCK: He did?

SERVANT: Yes, my lord. He said he did not want you to lose more than you actually have.

SHYLOCK: Oh...

(Enter Tudor)

TUDOR: Shylock! Shylock! I bring excellent new

SHYLOCK: What is it?

TUDOR: The ships which belonged to the merchant Antonio have been destroyed and he has no way to pay you the money back,

SHYLOCK: Ah! It is indeed an excellent news. God has been kind to me. I have lost a daughter but I have gained something even better. *(To his servant)* You! Lock the doors and head for home.

TUDOR: What about you?

SHYLOCK: I? I will go to that bastard and shall have my pound of flesh as promised.

(*Exeunt*)

SCENE 4

(A Court in Venice. Shouts, cries and curses are heard)

JUDGE: (Bangs his hammer on the table)Silence! Silence! This court demands silence.

(The court gets silent)

JUDGE: This court is summoned today to take up the case of the Christian Antonio and the Jew Shylock. Shylock & Antonio come forward.

(Shylock and Antonio enter)

JUDGE: Shylock this court once again pleads you to look into your bond and its terms

SHYLOCK: Why my Lord?

JUDGE: If the terms of your bond are carried out then poor Antonio may end up losing his precious life

SHYLOCK: My Lord. Antonio should have thought twice before signing the bond. His overconfidence brought him here and that is the reason of his death

JUDGE: And you Antonio? You have nothing to say in this situation?

ANTONIO: None, my Lord.

JUDGE: Then we shall proceed with the proceedings

(Shouts and cries are heard. Bassanio and Gratiano enter)

ANTONIO: Bassanio!

BASSANIO: Antonio my friend. I have arrived (*To Shylock*) And for you monster, I have brought the money which is more important to you than human life

SHYLOCK: That doesn't matter. The term period has ended. I will accept nothing else other than the pound of flesh that has been promised to me

BASSANIO: But?

ANTONIO: Forget it, dear Bassanio. Nothing can move the evil Jew other than the pound of flesh in his arms. Give me your hand so that I can hold you once again before I leave this mortal plane

BASSANIO: Please forgive me my friend as it is for me you have to go through such atrocities.

ANTONIO: Don't apologise dear friend for I don't blame you. Nothing brings me more happiness than knowing that I will be dying for you.

JUDGE: As it is stated in the bond the Jew Shylock will have his pound of flesh as he deserves and he shall get

Halt!!!

(Two young beautiful boys dressed in lawyer's attire walk-in)

JUDGE: You two who enter this court. State your names

BALTHAZAR: I am Balthazar and this is my clerk, my lord. We are here on behalf of Bellario. We wish to take up the case of the Jew Shylock and the Christian Antonio

JUDGE: If that is the case both of them are right in front of you

BALTHAZAR: May I see the bond?

SHYLOCK: It is here.

BALTHAZAR: It is said that Antonio was supposed to give a pound of flesh to Shylock if he could not pay the money back in a month's time. Were you able to Lord Antonio?

ANTONIO: I wasn't able to

BALTHAZAR: Then I don't see the issue that prevails. Shylock shall have the pound of flesh that he deserves

SHYLOCK: An upright lawyer. Prepare my knife and the scales and I shall my pound of flesh

(Brings a knife and the scales and gets ready to take the flesh)

BALTHAZAR: Halt!

SHYLOCK: Now what?

BALTHAZAR: You can take the pound of flesh that was promised to you but there was nothing written about the blood

SHYLOCK: What does that mean?

BALTHAZAR: That means that while taking the flesh if you drop a single Christian blood on the floor, you will be executed for murder. Also, if you take a bit more than a pound all your belongings shall be taken away from you.

(A roar of laughter and applause erupts in the court)

BASSANIO: You were right, Shylock. She is an upright judge

(Shylock stays silent for a while and then grabs the knife again)

SHYLOCK: Bring the Christian here. An opportunity like this can't be missed.

BASSANIO: You monster just how much do you hate us Christians to go to this extent

SHYLOCK: Hate you? How can I not? You Christians act all high and mighty and look down on us Jews. You don't miss an opportunity to belittle us. You insult us whenever you want just because we don't believe like you do and now you call me a monster. (Chuckles) Oh! The irony. I may be killed or have my possession taken but I might be able to take one of you down with me

BALTHAZAR: Shylock your hatred for us is understandable but you won't get anything from this.

SHYLOCK: Silence you vermin. You don't know my pain. These Christians took away my daughter from me too.

BALTHAZAR: Your daughter is happy with a Christian. If she can be, why can't you?

SHYLOCK: Because love has blinded her!!!!

ANTONIO: Her love hasn't blinded her. It has saved her. Your hatred on the other hand has blinded you.

SHYLOCK: Silence!!!!

BALTHAZAR: Your daughter. You will never be able to see her again

SHYLOCK: I don't want to see that ungrateful wretch anyway. Now where's my knife?

BALTHAZAR: How will your daughter when she finds out her father died because her father could not forgive the Christians? Jessica herself told me how she wishes her father forgave the Christians and look at them the way she sees them

SHYLOCK: How do you know all of that?

BALTHAZAR: Because I met your daughter on the way here. And I could see the care in her eyes. Don't betray the one person who cares for you, Shylock.

(Shylock stares at his knife)

BASSANIO: Jew no, Shylock I know we haven't been on the best of terms. But please forgive Antonio. Open your heart to Antonio and let us open our hearts to you.

(Bassanio offers his hand for a handshake and Shylock stares at it for a few moments. The court goes silent as if waiting for Shylock to react. Finally, Shylock clasps Bassanio's hand. The court erupts in cheers)

JUDGE:*(Bangs his hammer on the table)* Silence! This is still a court. Silence!!

(The court goes silent once again)

SHYLOCK: I will try

BASSANIO: *(Hugs Shylock)* That's all we need

BALTHAZAR: Then we shall take leave

ANTONIO: Please wait I still have to thank you

BALTHAZAR: Patience Lord Antonio we shall meet soon you can thank me then

ANTONIO: I do not understand

BALTHAZAR: You shall soon as for you Shylock your daughter waits for you in Belmont under Lady Portia's hospitality

BASSANIO: My wife! Let me take you, their Shylock. Antonio, you should also meet my beloved

BALTHAZAR: Then we shall leave for the next case that needs our assistance

ANTONIO: Thanks

(Balthazar and his clerk exit)

ANTONIO: A kind young man

BASSANIO: Yes indeed, but it feels as if I have met him before. Or have seen him before

SHYLOCK: You have

BASSANIO: Who knows? It is a small world. But for now, let's leave with haste for Belmont and my wife call us

SHYLOCK: So, does my daughter

(Exeunt)

SCENE 5

(A Castle in Belmont. Enter Bassanio, Antonio, Shylock)

BASSANIO: Welcome my friend to my wife's holy abode

SHYLOCK: It's a beautiful house. A house fitting for a lady like her

ANTONIO: You are right Shylock. It is indeed a beautiful house and the beauty of the lady so far, I have heard outmatches the house.

BASSANIO: That it does

(Enter Portia)

PORTIA: Welcome to my holy abode gentlemen

BASSANIO:*(Kisses her)* And this is my wife

ANTONIO: Hello Lady Portia. I must say the rumours of your beauty do not do justice to your beauty

SHYLOCK: You speak the truth, dear Antonio

PORTIA: Lord Antonio Lord Shylock it is good to see Bassanio has told me so much about you two

SHYLOCK: I can't wait to hear what all Bassanio has talked about me

(Everyone laughs)

BASSANIO: Lady Portia, a young lawyer named Balthazar told me that my daughter Jessica is here with you.

PORTIA: Why yes Lord Shylock she should come out any moment

(Enter Jessica with Lorenzo following her)

SHYLOCK:*(Rushes forward and hugs her)* I thought I had lost you forever.

(Jessica starts crying)

SHYLOCK: Why did you run away?

JESSICA: I thought you would never accept my love for Lorenzo because he is a Christian

SHYLOCK: Yes, I would not have but now *(Looks at Antonio and Bassanio)* my views have changed. *(To Lorenzo)* You come forward

(Lorenzo comes forward)

SHYLOCK: My servants told me how you told Jessica not to take the jewels with her

LORENZO: That I did sir

SHYLOCK: The past me would have never acknowledged this feat of yours but the present me can see your true nature. I hope you can keep my daughter happy, happier than I ever could

LORENZO: I would try my best sir

SHYLOCK:*(To Antonio)* I would like to help you with losses you have incurred due to losing your ships. You can take the three thousand ducats which you owe me.

ANTONIO: My friend I don't know how to thank you

SHYLOCK: There is no need for that. I just wish I could thank the young lawyer who stopped me from killing you

JESSICA: You could thank him here since he him in this room

(All look around confused as Portia begins to giggle)

PORTIA: Didn't I tell you, Lord Antonio that we will meet again soon

ANTONIO: My lady, how did you?

BASSANIO: My love, how did you?

PORTIA: Easy love. All questions and confusion will be answered and cleared. Let's go inside where I will reveal it all amidst food and drinks

(Exeunt)

VI
THE STORY OF NIHARA - DEVANANDA S KURUP

SCENE 1

(The story starts in the dense forest of Kurkail. The chirping of birds. Enter Bheem, Dhwani and some tribal teenagers.)

BHEEM: Dhwani, you are so beautiful!

DHWANI: Thank you, so do you.

DHOL: So do you?

(Everyone laughs mockingly)

DHWANI: What's there to laugh at?

DHOL: You are saying this because you haven't seen any other men other than us.

DHWANI: Men other than you people, don't fool me.

DHOL: No Dhwani, other men and women besides us look completely different.

DHWANI: Different?

DHOL: They wear clothes made of fabric, and ornaments out of gold and they don't mark their face with soot.

DHWANI: Don't lie to me! Bheem, is he telling the truth?

BHEEM: There are other humans besides us but that doesn't make us less beautiful *(stares at Dhol)*

DHOL: I can show you my friend who is not from our forest

BHEEM:*(to Dhol angrily)* What are you up to?

DHWANI: Really! When can I meet him?

DHOL: He often comes here in the afternoon for hunting, so probably he will come after a few hours.

(Everyone exits)

(Afternoon time. Enter Dhol and Dhruv, prince of Acharya in another part of the forest.)

DHOL: How are you, my friend?

DHRUV: Nothing much Dhol. What about you?

DHOL: One of my friends wants to meet you.

DHRUV: Meet me!?

DHOL: Can you come with me?

DHRUV: oh sure

(Both walk through the forest and Dhruv sees Dhwani sitting by the river. Enter Dhwani)

DHRUV: *(shockingly)* Who is she? Is she a goddess?

DHOL: No. That's my friend who wanted to see you.

(Dhwani sees Dhruv and both instantly fall in love.)

SCENE 2

(Enter Mahespati and Harsh sitting in the courtroom with other royals. The Minister comes running.)

MINISTER: My Lord our Prince hasn't returned

MAHESPATI: Dhruv! Where did he go?

HARSH: As usual he would be roaming here and there with his horse *(said mockingly)*

MINISTER: No my lord, it's been some time since he left. Usually, it doesn't take him this much time. I think something might have happened

MAHESHPATI: Has he not told where he has gone?

HARSH: He would have gone to the enemy empire to plot against his father... *(in a loud voice sarcastically)*

MAHESHPATI: *(Scolding Harsh)* Let it be the last time! *(To minister)* Do you have any clue of where Dhruv usually goes for hunting?

MINISTER: As he was getting bored of the hunting Spots. His intentions and courage speak to him to go to the mysterious forest of Kurkail for the last hunt. I am fearful to share with you that he went to that place where no courageous men came back from...

(The whole crowd in the court went to silence. King was beyond words for a while)

HARSH: Even the most valorous men haven't returned from this forest so what do you expect of this wimp?

MAHESHPATI: Stop this at once Harsh. It is my son who is missing and I am going to find him and you are coming with me.

(Exit Mahespati, Harsh and others)

SCENE 3

(Enter Dhruv and Dhwani sitting under a banyan admiring each other.)

DHRUV: If there is heaven on Earth my lady it will be you (*Dhwani blushes*)

DHWANI: Oh please you are flattering me

DHRUV: Oh love, I thought you were the goddess Parvati who came to bless me.

DHWANI: Dear first I didn't believe what Dhol said because I haven't seen any other men apart from them

DHRUV: What about your father?

(Enter Aadhya, Bheem and other guards)

AADHYA: Who is this boy? (*Both stand in shock and fear*)

DHWANI: Maa, he is Dhruv

AADHYA: Dhruv?

DHRUV: (*as a proud warrior says*) I am Dhruv the prince of Acharya the son of the great king Mahespati.

(Aadhya looked at him in surprise)

AADHYA: Are you really the son of that monster

DHWANI: Mother!

AADHYA: Dhwani you don't know what his father has done to us.

DHWANI: But, He's innocent.

AADHYA: Don't be deceived by looks Dhwani, All that glitters is not gold.

(Dhruv is surprised and doesn't know what is happening)

DHRUV: Madam, What have I done? Why do you hate my father so much?

AADHYA: *(In anger)* Get out of my sight, you will not leave this island until I permit you. From now onwards you are my servant.

(Aadhya assigns difficult jobs for Dhruv which questions his royalty, Dhruv who is in love with Dhwani accepts it willingly. Dhruv exits)

AADHYA: Dear Dhwani, you might not remember this. How could you, you were just some months old. As him, you are also a princess of the great kingdom Nihara and I the Queen.

DHWANI: Stop lying mother.

AADHYA: Your uncle Hreedhan spread a rumour on your birth that you are a curse to the kingdom and with the help of the neighbouring kingdom that is Dhruv's kingdom they attacked Nihara one night and killed your father, hearing this I ran from the palace with you through the secret chamber where our minister had arranged a horse for us and thus we came to this lovely person who welcomed us and made me their leader.

DHWANI: Oh dear mother I didn't know you went through all this. But why are you punishing him? He doesn't know about this.

AADHYA: Dhwani, I know you love that young man but we don't know if this is just out of excitement as you are seeing a man apart from this island for the first time and I don't believe his father's blood can bear something good so we should test whether his love is pure or not. And so you are forbidden even to see him unless I give you permission.

(Exits Aadhya and Dhwani)

SCENE 4

(Mahespati and his company go through the mystical forest of Kurkail on horseback and in between their journey they get split into two groups.)

(Enter Mahespati and his accompany)

MAHESHPATI: Oh dear God, what have I done to deserve all this? Please keep my boy safe.

HARSH: *(Aside)* Oh boy here we go again. That whiner must have already been dead. Shall I just push him off the horse into the thorny shrubs and be the next king...

MAHESPATI: Harsh are you here?

(King and Hreedhan looks back and to their surprise, they find that Bala and Viraj are missing)

HREEDHAN: My lord, where are the others?

MAHESPATI: Oh God, what is happening in this mysterious forest

(To Harsh) stay alert dear boy, I don't want to lose you either.

(Exit Mahespati, Harsh, Hreedhan.)

(Enter Bala and Viraj.)

BALA: Where are the others?

VIRAJ: Seems like we are lost. Who cares, as long as I have my divine drink with me?

(Enter Bheem) (Bheem was roaming around the forest)

BALA: *(To Bheem)* Hey you, come here.

(Bheem ignores Bala and walks away.)

VIRAJ: Hey young man please come here.

BHEEM: What do you want your old geezers?

VIRAJ: Could you please help us? We are lost in this mysterious forest.

BHEEM: What would I get in return?

BALA: Viraj it will be of no good asking this fool for help. I'd rather stay here and die.

BHEEM: *(To Bala)* Shut your mouth or I'll tear you in pieces you old geezer.

VIRAJ: Both of you stop. Young man, please help us and in return for this favour, I'll give you this whole bottle of my divine drink which is very dear to me. Here, have a sip.

VIRAJ: Gives the bottle to Bheem and he drinks it.

BHEEM: Oh dear lord what is this some magical drink straight out of heaven or what? Good master whatever you need I'll help you.

VIRAJ: No need to call me master just call me by my name. Viraj.

BHEEM: No my lord. From now on you are my master. I'll serve you for the rest of my life. I do not want to be under the rule of that wrecked witch Aadhya Devi

BALA: Is she still alive?

BHEEM: Yes

(To Viraj) Dear lord if you wish I can make you the ruler of this land by killing her but I only have one condition.

VIRAJ: What is it?

BHEEM: She has a daughter named Dhwani who is very beautiful and I want to marry her.

(Both of them get into a pact. Exits Bala, Viraj and Bheem)

• 51 •

SCENE 5

(Dhruv was splitting wood and carrying logs and then Dhwani came in.)

DHWANI: Oh dear lord you are suffering all this torture for me.

DHRUV: Love, this is not suffering as long as I am doing this for you.

DHWANI: Please don't tell my mother that I came here.

DHRUV: Why would I?

(Hears the trotting of horses.)

DHRUV: *(In surprise)* That noise.

(Enter Mahespati, Harsh and Hreedhan.)

MAHESHPATI: *(In rush)* Son where were you? What are you doing and who is this girl?

DHRUV: Paapa, this is Dhwani, the love of my life.

HREEDHAN: *(To Dhwani)* You look familiar

(Suddenly Aadhya Devi enters.)

AADHYA: (in a furious tone) Haven't I warned you not to speak to him?

DHWANI: But maa... *(Hreedhan interrupts)*

HREEDHAN: Bhabhi

(Everyone looks astounded)

AADHYA: How dare you come here.

DHRUV: Paapa, What have we done? Why are they mad at us?

MAHESHPATI: She is the daughter of Dheeraj the former king of Vihara. I won't allow this marriage.

DHRUV: Why?

HARSH: You marrying her would curse our kingdom.

(Dhwani looks at Dhruv)

MAHESHPATI: Hreedhan had told us that she was born with a curse which would destroy the kingdom and that she would marry you and destroy our kingdom also that's why we tried to kill her.

Aadhya smirks.

AADHYA: *(To Hreedhan)* What all lies have you told?

(Mahespati understands that all of this was a lie and asks Aadhya Devi for forgiveness.)

MAHESHPATI: My Queen, because of this liar all this happened.

AADHYA: How do you expect me to forgive you when you killed my husband?

MAHESHPATI: Your husband is not dead.

(Everyone stares at him out of shock.)

AADHYA:What!

MAHESHPATI: He was imprisoned all this time. I didn't have the mind to kill him.

(Tears come from Aadhya's eyes.

Enter Bala, Viraj and Bheem)

VIRAJ: My Queen, you are alive. These drunkards were plotting to kill you.

(The tribal people there imprison both.)

MAHESHPATI: Please leave Bala. He utters nonsense when he is drunk, otherwise he is innocent.

DHRUV: *(To Mahespati and Aadhya Devi)* Can you please give us the consent to get married?

AADHYA: Get ready Dhwani. We are going back to our kingdom.

(Exeunt)

VII
A ROYAL ENCOUNTER - GRACE GETHSIBA S

SCENE 1

(In Rome, the Triumvirate are expecting the arrival of Cairo, the King of Egypt. Since Cairo couldn't make it so he sent his wife Cleopatra in his stead.)

ANTONY: They must be here by now, shouldn't they?

LEPIDUS: Calm down, mate. They'll be here any moment now. Oh! Look here they come.

(Cleopatra and her people enter)

ANTONY: I thought we were expecting King Cairo. Could this be his wife?

OCTAVIUS: Hush now brother and smile. The triumvirate welcomes you to Rome. Octavius Caesar. And you are Lady….? (*Extends his hand*)

CLEOPATRA:(*Places her hand on his*) Cleopatra. Wife of Cairo. I'm here in his stead, he apologises for being unable to make it for certain reasons.

LEPIDUS: Lepidus, my Lady. It's wonderful to meet you. (*Kisses her hand*)

ANTONY: Mark Antony. *(Kisses her hand)* I hope you enjoy your stay in Rome, my Lady.

I will escort you to your room.

CLEOPATRA: *(Blushes)* Such a gentleman! *(Aside)* Why do I find myself attracted to Octavius and Antony simultaneously?

(Cleopatra gets into trysts with Antony and Octavius but both men are unaware of it. One day Antony visits Octavius in his chamber and finds his lover there.)

ANTONY: Oh my God! *(Shocked)* Why are you both in the same room? My Lady, I thought you loved me, now you're with Octavius?

OCTAVIUS: *(Confused)* Wait! What do you mean by love you? Had she been with you before me? My dear, tell me it's not true!!

CLEOPATRA: *(Stands between them)* Octavius, I wish it wasn't true. What can I do if my heart has fallen for both of you?

ANTONY: So you mean that you love us both?

CLEOPATRA: Yes! I love you both equally. Oh, Antony, Octavius! Your countenances are so fine and fierce that it makes me wonder if the Gods in heaven have sculpted you with their own hands. *(Kisses them both).*

ANTONY: *(Embraces her)* You, my dear, truly are a work of art. You're like the beautiful flowers in the field.

OCTAVIUS: *(Embraces her)* I would do anything for you, dear. I would even sail to the end of the world for you. We're fine with your decision.

(Exeunt)

SCENE 2

(Word has travelled to Cairo that his wife is having an affair with Antony and Octavius, enraged by this news he plans to take revenge. Conversely, Pompey Rome's rival is eager to bring down the mighty Triumvirate and uses this to his advantage and seeks Cairo's alliance.)

(Pompey's palace. In the throne room. Pompey enters along with Varrius)

POMPEY: This is the right time to bring the Triumvirate down. Don't you think, Varrius?

VARRIUS: Sire, how can it be so? Have you got any plans in mind?

POMPEY: Of course, I do. The triumvirate is invincible and nothing can be used against them, but this time there's someone very dear to them.

VARRIUS: Do you mean the lady lover, Your Majesty?

POMPEY: Yes, Varrius. The very same lady lover whom Antony and Octavius are fond of. I believe she's their weakness and I will use her to get them.

VARRIUS: But, Your Majesty! Don't you know who she is? She's not an ordinary woman like you think.

POMPEY: What are you saying Varrius? Could you be clear?

VARRIUS: The lady lover is none other than Cleopatra, the Egyptian Queen.

POMPEY: (*Astounded*) Cleopatra? King Cairo's spouse? We must not involve her in our plan of bringing the triumvirate down, or we would have to face the wrath of Cairo.

VARRIUS: Sire. Why don't we make Egypt our ally and seek help from the King? He has a powerful army; after all, he would want revenge against the men who stole his wife.

POMPEY: Good idea Varrius, my most loyal advisor. Send King Cairo a letter stating that we'll be visiting him soon.

VARRIUS: Yes, Sire. I will at once.

(Varrius exits)

POMPEY: I hope this plan doesn't fail us.

(A week later a letter arrives to Cleopatra saying her husband is dead, immediately she starts preparing for her departure to Egypt. That same night, at the harbour the triumvirate arrived to say goodbye.)

OCTAVIUS: Have a safe journey, my dear. (He kisses her and embraces her)

CLEOPATRA: Thank you, Octavius. I'll miss you.

LEPIDUS: (*Embraces her and kisses her on the cheek*) Hope everything goes well, my Lady.

CLEOPATRA: Thank you Lepidus, I hope so too.

ANTONY: (*Fake cries*) Are you not going to miss me?

CLEOPATRA: (*Chuckles*) I'm going to miss you too Antony. (*Embraces him and kisses him*)

(Iras enters)

IRAS: We're ready to depart, my Lady.

CLEOPATRA: (*Nods*) I'll be there.

IRAS: I'll take my leave, Your Highnesses.

(Iras exits)

CLEOPATRA: I'll take my leave too. Thank you so much for your hospitality, I had a wonderful time here in Rome. Goodbye. *(Bows)*

THE TRIUMVIRATE: *(Bows back)* Goodbye, Cleopatra.

(Exeunt)

SCENE 3

(A couple of months later Cleopatra returns to Rome after taking care of everything back in Egypt. One day her maidservant Iras comes weeping into her chamber.)

CLEOPATRA: What is wrong, Iras? Why are you crying?

IRAS:*(Falls at her feet sobbing)* I have betrayed you, my Lady.

CLEOPATRA: What? What have you done to betray me that I'm not aware of?

IRAS: The King, your husband, had ordered me to watch over everything you do here at Rome and report it to him.

CLEOPATRA: Why are you telling me this now? There's no use, he's dead.

IRAS: I needed to get it out of my chest, my Lady. The guilt was eating me up from inside and I

could bear it no more. I have a feeling that he might not be dead, maybe he's there somewhere!

(Quietly sobs)

CLEOPATRA: He is dead, Iras. I'm sure. It's just the guilt that's making you assume things like that.

IRAS: *(Nods)* No, my Lady. He was as cunning as the fox, no one could predict his next move. I don't deserve your forgiveness. I am a great sinner who betrayed her mistress. I am not worthy to live, please finish my life. *(Bends her head in shame)*

CLEOPATRA: *(Shocked. Stands up and places her hand on Iras' shoulders)* You're forgiven, Iras.

IRAS: *(Dumbstruck)* My Lady! Why? Why do you want to forgive a traitor such as me?

CLEOPATRA: I'm not like Cairo, Iras. He had a heart as hard as stone and cold as ice. Destruction was his way of doing things but not mine. Since you've confessed your mistakes, I think you deserve another chance. *(Smiles)*

IRAS:*(bows)* I will forever be grateful to you, my Lady.

CLEOPATRA: Go now, Iras. Go in peace.

(Iras exits)

(A couple of days later, Antony, Octavius and Cleopatra are lounging in the palace library when Atticus Lepidus' commander comes in with distressing news.)

CLEOPATRA: Oh God! (Laughs) It's been so long since I had a good laugh.

(Atticus enters)

ATTICUS: (Bows) Your Majesties, I am sorry to interrupt but you're being needed right away.

(Antony, Octavius and Cleopatra follow Atticus to one of the palace towers where they meet Lepidus.)

LEPIDUS: Thank god you guys are here! Take a look at that. *(Points towards the mountain region)*

ANTONY: It looks like a sandstorm. *(Gets punched in the arm by Octavius)* Ouch! What was that for?

OCTAVIUS: You fool! That's no sandstorm. Look carefully.

ANTONY: *(Squints his eyes)* Oh! You're right, that's not a sandstorm. Sorry, I've got a bad eyesight. *(Awkward laugh)*

LEPIDUS: *(Rolls his eyes)* This is no time to be joking around, Antony. It's an army of soldiers and they are approaching our way. They seem so familiar.

ATTICUS: That's because it is Sextus Pompey's army, Sire.

ANTONY: How could he wage a war when we are unprepared?

LEPIDUS: We cannot back down, mate. *(Angered)* We need to show him that Romans are not to be messed with.

OCTAVIUS: Atticus! Secure the city walls and tell Eros and Tarus to look after the rest. Prepare our men, we're going for battle.

ATTICUS: Yes, Sire.

(Atticus exits)

CLEOPATRA: *(In a worried tone)* Will you guys be fighting in the battle too?

ANTONY: Yes, darling. We have no choice, our men need us.

CLEOPATRA: Please return safely. Rome needs you. *(Embraces them)*

OCTAVIUS: We surely will, love. I want you to stay in your chamber till we return and do not come out. We have some men guarding the palace so there won't be any danger.

CLEOPATRA: *(Nods)* Okay.

ANTONY: We must leave now! Goodbye, love. *(Kisses her)*

(Antony exits)

OCTAVIUS: See you soon, beautiful. *(Kisses her)*

(Octavius exits)

LEPIDUS: Be safe, my Lady. *(Briefly bows)*

(Lepidus exits)

CLEOPATRA: *(Sighs)* Why do I feel like something's going to happen?

(Exeunt)

SCENE 4

(The Triumvirate were defeated in the war as Pompey had the Egyptian army on his side. Antony

and Octavius were captured while Lepidus escaped. On the very same day, Cairo whom everyone thought to be dead disguised himself as a Roman soldier and kidnapped Cleopatra taking her back to Egypt. Lepidus after coming to know of this, devices a plan to save the three of them. During this time two new relationships bloom between Iras and Lepidus and Charmain and Eros - Antony's commander.)

(In Pompey's palace. In the cell.)

ANTONY: *(Huffs)* Why is nobody coming to get us, brother?

OCTAVIUS: Patience, Antony, patience. *(Sighs)* You've seriously got no patience.

ANTONY: How can you stand being in this dark and dirty dungeon? I'm a germaphobe and yet that idiot has put me here.

OCTAVIUS: Oh please! Stop complaining I can't take it.

(The sound of footsteps approaching)

ANTONY: Shhh.... *(Places his finger on his lips)* Can you hear that? Someone's coming. Maybe someone's coming to rescue us.

OCTAVIUS: *(Places his palm on his forehead and shakes his head)* Oh, God!!

(The sound of footsteps gets closer)

(Lepidus enters)

LEPIDUS: Hello brothers. Missed me? *(Wiggles his eyebrows)*

OCTAVIUS: Lepidus, my brother! Thank God you're here. Please save me from this dumb head. *(Points to Antony)*

ANTONY: I'm not a dumb head. I told you someone would come to rescue us and I was right!

LEPIDUS: Keep your voices down, we need to get out of here before someone comes. *(Breaks the lock and enters the cell. Breaks the chains)* Quick! Keep moving.

(A clash takes place between the Romans and Pompey's men. Pompey is killed by Lepidus. The Romans march to Egypt after knowing that Cairo has faked his death and has Cleopatra. A few days later, in Alexandria, Cairo lies relaxing and sipping wine in his chamber when his commander comes panicked.)

CAIRO: Ah! What a wonderful day it is! *(Twirls the wine in the glass and downs it)*

(Karim enters)

KARIM: My Lord! We're under attack!

CAIRO: What? By whom?

KARIM: *(Gulps)* The Romans.

CAIRO: What? *(Drops his glass in bewilderment)* No, that's impossible. Two of them are held captives and no one knows about the other.

KARIM: All the three of them are here, My Lord. What do we do?

CAIRO:*(Frantically moves his hands as he yells)* Do something!!

(Karim exits)

(The maidservants, Charmian and Iras secretly enter the dungeons to rescue Cleopatra only to find that she doesn't look like herself at all – pale, skinny and lifeless. They help her get out of the dungeon when a soldier stops them)

SOLDIER: What are you doing? She's supposed to be in the dungeon. *(Points to Cleopatra)*

(The maidservants look at each other as Eros enters knocking out the soldier)

EROS: *(Motions his hand)* Let's go!

CHARMIAN: *(Smiles)* Thank you.

EROS: No problem my lady. *(Returns a smile)*

(Eros leads the three of them out to the palace gardens while a duo takes place between Octavius and Cairo inside. Cairo kills Octavius by stabbing him and in return, Antony kills Cairo as an act of revenge. Octavius is then brought to Cleopatra and takes his last breath on his lover's lap.)

(Exeunt)

SCENE 5

(A few months later, in the palace of Rome, inside Antony's chamber Lepidus, the Generals and the maidservants are gathered.)

LEPIDUS: How have you been, my Lady?

CLEOPATRA: Lepidus! I am much better, thank you. How are things going in Egypt?

LEPIDUS: All is well, my Lady. Iras and I have something to tell you all. *(Intertwines his hand with Iras)* We are getting married!!

ANTONY: Wow! Really? Congratulations, brother. *(Embraces him)* Congratulations, Iras.

IRAS: Thank you, Your Highness. My Lady, I want to seek your blessing. Even after I betrayed you, you still gave me another chance and I am very thankful for that. I will never forget your kindness.

CLEOPATRA: Iras. *(Holds Iras' hand)* I give you my blessings. May you live long and happy.

IRAS: *(Kisses her hand)* Thank you, my Lady.

ANTONY: What are you guys doing here? *(Points to Charmian and the generals)* Are you planning on getting married again?

EROS: *(Startled)* What? No, Sire. Never.

CHARMIAN:*(In a threatening tone)* Even if he does, I will not spare him till I break each bone in his body.

(Everyone breaks into laughter. Eros and Charmian hold hands and kneel on one knee.)

EROS: We're expecting a child soon.

CLEOPATRA: *(Smiles in excitement)* A child!! That's such wonderful news. Congratulations to both of you.

LEPIDUS: Congratulations! Is it a boy or a girl?

CHARMIAN: We don't know the gender yet but we've decided the name. If it's a boy, he'll be named Octavius.

EROS: If it's a girl, she'll be named Cleopatra.

CLEOPATRA: *(Shedding happy tears)* I don't know what to say. I wish he was here right now, he would be so happy.

(A sombre feeling settles in the chamber)

ANTONY: *(Embraces Cleopatra)* Love, he's always here. *(Looks up)* I believe he's up there looking down on us and rejoicing.

(Exeunt)

VIII
REBELLION IN THE CORPORATE WORLD - HAOBAM NISHITA

(A realm of business where power dynamics and ambition collide. As the drama unfolds, witness the clash between tradition and change.)

SCENE 1

(The stage is set with sleek desks, buzzing with activity and the glow of computer screens. Lucifer, the CEO of a renowned retail company addresses internal issues. His son, Bruce enters)

LUCIFER: As we all know, our product sales have been drastically decreasing for the past few months and according to some employees seated here with us, we were informed that our partnership with Clark Company has been shut down due to some issues.

BRUCE: What may be the issue?

LUCIFER: Harris, the CEO of Clark Company has been constantly trying to evoke conflict with us and it is most likely that our company might collapse in the next coming years since their products are way more developed compared to ours.

BRUCE: Conflict? For what? That is ridiculous.

LUCIFER: No one knows the reason why he's doing all these things. But whatever the reason may be, we must ensure not to engage with such conflicts with them that might lead us to our downfall.

BRUCE: (*nodding his head*) I will certainly try my best to look into it. (*Talking to himself*) Maybe he had other reasons? God knows.

(Bruce quickly exits through the door)

SCENE 2

(The stage is set with tables and chairs. There, few employees are being seated and it can be observed that they're discussing the ongoing situation. Bruce enters)

CHRIS (EMPLOYEE 1): Harris, that darn wretch. I wonder what he's up to now. I used to work in his company and I must admit, their product sales are quite high compared to other companies.

JOHN (EMPLOYEE 2): So, do you have any idea on what the actual issue is?

CHRIS: I'm not sure but they have a knack for finding ways to challenge and provoke their competitors.

JOHN: Like?

CHRIS: Like aggressive marketing campaigns, undercutting prices, or even poaching employees.

BRUCE: (*laughs*) Well, seems like we got a lot in our hands to deal with this so-called Harris of ours aye?

LIAM (EMPLOYEE 3): We must do something Sir. We can't let their antics ruin our reputation.

BRUCE: Calm down Liam. All we need to make sure is staying true to our values. It's actually stupid to get caught up in unnecessary conflicts.

JOHN: Agreed Sir. We can monitor their actions and by adapting our strategies, we can proactively respond to any challenges they pose.

BRUCE: Good point, John! That is exactly what I was looking for. For now, let's focus on what our CEO is planning to do with all this mess.

(Everyone shook hands with one another and exits)

SCENE 3

(This scene takes place in a sleek, high-rise office building. Harris enters boastfully and sits on one of the chairs. Bruce and his employees enters)

HARRIS: *raising an eyebrow with a smirk*) Well well, Mr. Bruce, I must say, your way of managing this company is truly impressive. Your strategic decisions are as innovative as a fax machine in the digital age. Bravo!

BRUCE: (*smiling confidently with a touch of amusement*) Ah yes Mr. Harris, your words may sting, but they only fuel my determination to prove you wrong. While you revel in your clever insults, I'll be busy leading my father's company towards greatness.

HARRIS: (*chuckling*) Oh Mr. Bruce, how admirable it is that you find solace in your delusions under your father's company.

BRUCE: Tell me, Mr. Harris, what drives your relentless pursuit of undermining our company? Is it a thirst for power or a deep-rooted desire to prove your own worth?

HARRIS: How fascinating it is that you're suddenly interested in understanding me. I must say, your curiosity is truly overwhelming. But don't worry, I won't keep you waiting for long. My drive to surpass you and achieve greatness is simply unmatched.

(The employees are shown getting tensed)

BRUCE: (*smiling*) You see, I've stumbled upon certain information that could be quite damaging to your reputation.

HARRIS: Oh, is it?

BRUCE: Ah yes. Unethical business practices, manipulation of financial records and even poaching employees? Wow Mr. Harris, you do know that this information might cause some negative consequences for your company, right?

HARRIS: So you think you've got me cornered huh? Don't underestimate my ability to handle this situation. I'll do whatever it takes to protect my reputation and come out on top.

BRUCE: Well it seems your deceitful ways have caught up with you. (*Showing him all the articles and news on his phone*) The evidence against you is as clear as daylight. Because of my smart fellow employees and their loyalties, we were able to track down all your dirty little tricks.

HARRIS: (*clenching his fist and tries to stay calm*) So, you think you've won, Mr. Bruce? Don't celebrate just yet. Be ashamed that you're still under your father's company and acting all high on me.

BRUCE: Oh Mr. Harris, it's better if you worry about your reputation instead. Shaming my father's company won't bring your company any better. Keep your threats to yourself.

(Harries gets a call and he immediately exits through the door and all the employees got up and went to praise Bruce for his leadership and confidence.)

SCENE 4

(Lucifer enters)

LUCIFER: I knew you would handle it well. After all, you're my son.

BRUCE: (*laughs*) Now where were you all these time?

LUCIFER: I was enjoying the drama of course. (laughs). But yes, don't let all that fury rattle you. Stay strong and focus on your path to success. Remember, you have the intelligence and resilience to overcome any challenge that comes your way.

(Bruce finds comfort in his father's words, knowing that he has the support and wisdom of a true mentor.

With this, both the son and father embarked on a journey to boost sales and improve customer relationships through effective retail strategies like upselling and suggestive selling.)

(Exeunt)

IX
THE NIGHT WE MET - HELEN LALREMPUII SAILO

SCENE 1

(Thunder, lightning, raining and whining)

AMANDA: *(padding her dad)* Papa, everything will be fine.

HECTOR: We'll get to see mom again in heaven papa, don't worry.

TAMANNA: *(Callie holding Tamanna's hand)* Rest well Mama.

(As Callie looks up she sees a man with a blurred face and wakes up from her dreams)

(Birds chirping, Amanda entering Callie's room)

AMANDA: Rise and shine sister!! *(Suddenly stop)* you okay? You're sweating.

CALLIE: Absolutely fine, just a dream.

AMANDA: Nightmares again!? Tell me.

CALLIE: No, everything is fine. It's just a dream.

AMANDA: You sure? Okay.

CALLIE: Yea sure.

AMANDA: I bet you dreamed of mom again.

CALLIE: (*smirk*) I mean yes, can't hide. You know me well.

AMANDA: We all miss Mama.

(They both went out of the room and started their day.)

SCENE 2

(As midnight has come as usual the bar is full again.)

SOLDIER 1: Heyyyy Hoooo!!!! The night has come my dearest friends. What we longed for has come tonight.

SOLDIER 2: Let us all raise and toss!!!

SOLDIER 1: Let us all welcome all our new sepoys who had joined us tonight, who had served this country and fought for freedom. Cheers!!

SOLDIER 3: Play the music, let's dance and shake the night off. Haiiiyaaaaaa!!!

(Everybody getting drunk and dancing)

BRUNO: Let me fill up your cups, my brother.

HAROLD: (*smiling*) Always on set, my brother.

BRUNO: Trust me, the ladies here tonight are hot! You better try talking to one.

HAROLD: (*laughing*) Let's see if I can pull one. Should we order another bottle? Ready for another round?

BRUNO: Haiyaaaa!! Let's go.

(As Harold lead forward to the counter and saw Callie, he caught his eyes)

HAROLD: Hello, Mrs. Beautiful.

(Callie blushing)

CALLIE: May I help you, Sire?

HAROLD: Would you mind giving me another bottle?

CALLIE: My pleasure, I'll serve you.

HAROLD: Table number 9. I'll wait patiently.

CALLIE: Got it.

(As Callie served them, Bruno was more excited than Harold)

CALLIE: Here, enjoy your drinks.

BRUNO: Would you mind sitting with us? Because such a beautiful lady like you sitting with us is a win-win. Is it not, brother?

HAROLD: I hope so *(blushing as he look at Callie)*

CALLIE: How can I resist such words from knights like you.

HAROLD: Hi, my name is Harold and this is my friend Bruno.

CALLIE: Nice to meet you two. My name is Callie.

HAROLD: Callie *(looking at her, slowly calling her name)* what a nice name. So, Callie, you work here or what?

CALLIE: Haha, my dad is the owner of this bar.

HAROLD: Ohhh woww, okay that's a surprise.

CALLIE: What's so surprising there?

HAROLD: Nothing *(blushing as he look down)*

BRUNO: So Callie, it's our first time coming here. Would you suggest places to visit?

CALLIE: Sure why not.

BRUNO: Do you have a boyfriend or are you already married?

CALLIE: *(sarcastically laughing)* Of course not.

(Both Harold and Bruno starred at each other and smile)

HAROLD: I wish to see you more often, Callie.

CALLIE: No worries, I'm staying here.

SCENE 3

(Patrick coming home from his long travelled)

HECTOR: Papa will reach soon, I'm so excited. We finally got the chance to stay together again, TAMANNA.

TAMANNA: Right!!! Papa is finally coming home. Is the food ready? Callie, have you made the chicken soup? Papa's favourite.

CALLIE: Of course my dear. All are set.

AMANDA: Papa!! Guysss dad is here!!! He's here.

(As they all ran towards their dad, hugging and laughing)

HECTOR: I miss so much, Papa.

PATRICK: I miss you all too. Come let's not just stand here and go. I'm hungry, I can smell chicken soup

(All laughing)

(The next day)

PATRICK: Come here my dear.

(Callie sitting next to her dad)

So how's the bar? Everything was fine while I was gone, right?

CALLIE: Sure Papa everything was fine.

PATRICK: That's good to hear. Ever since your mom left, as you are the oldest, all these have come to be your responsibility. I'm so proud of you seeing you manage to take care of the bar and your siblings. You've come a great way, my dear.

CALLIE: It's all I can do. I wish I could do more.

(Callie watering the plants)

HAROLD: I didn't expect to see you here, Callie.

CALLIE: Hello Harold, what are you doing here?

HAROLD: Was just passing by. To have a good view.

CALLIE: Okay, I see.

HAROLD: Is this your farm?

CALLIE: As you can see, yes.

HAROLD: So, ummm any special program tonight?

CALLIE: No

HAROLD: Can we go out for dinner? If you don't mind.

CALLIE: I'm honoured to hear that.

HAROLD: I take that as a Yes.

CALLIE: Sure.

HAROLD: 7:30 p.m., okay?

CALLIE: okay.

HAROLD: The Wagner Restaurant, I'll be there for you.

(Harold patiently waits for Callie to come. After few minutes Callie has arrived)

HAROLD: Thank you for coming.

CALLIE: I told you I'll come (*smirk*)

(*Both smiling*)

HAROLD: You are beautiful. I thought I saw an angel for a second.

CALLIE: Hahaha stop it.

(After one year of being in a relationship, they even plan to marry. One day a letter came from The General)

PATRICK: Amanda, where is your sister Callie? Is Harold not coming to have dinner with us?

AMANDA: They both went shopping, don't worry Papa, they will be home soon. Harold will stay with us tonight.

PATRICK: Okay that's good to hear. I miss them both.

AMANDA: They will be home soon.

HECTOR: Have you made the chicken soup? I'm becoming more like my dad now.

(All laughing)

TAMANNA: Of course! Everything is ready. We now only wait for Harold and Callie.

(Harold and Callie had arrived and they all had their dinner together)

HAROLD: The dish was super.

TAMANNA: See Papa I know Harold would like it.

PATRICK: Haha so proud of you dear. Just like your mom, you're good at cooking. I know Amanda is capable of doing it too.

(As Harold left and reached his house, there was a letter in his letter box. The letter from The General has arrived. The next day Harold and Callie meet again.)

HAROLD: Callie (*calling her dully*)

CALLIE: Yes, what is it? You seemed down.

HAROLD: I got a letter last night. Letter from 'The General Baldwin'. He requested me to join the army again. What should I do, Callie? I couldn't leave you alone as well as how can I leave this country? The dilemma I'm facing right now, Callie.

CALLIE: I want to spend the rest of my life with you. I've chosen you. I want you to stay. But what can I say Harold. It's for the country. Go serve for the country and make us proud. I'll wait for you patiently.

(Harold has left and served for the country)

SCENE 4

(After five years. It's summer noon, Callie as usual is writing a letter for Harold, everyday she's waiting for Harold's letter. But till date Harold never sent one)

AMANDA: Here, have your launch please.

CALLIE: Thank you, Amanda.

AMANDA: You're still writing for him?

(Callie smiling)

AMANDA: I want you to wake up please. We don't know if he's still alive or dead. We don't know if he has already started a new life. Stop waiting, stop writing him a letter which we don't know if he received it or not or ignoring it. Please for the sake of mom and dad get a new life.

CALLIE: How do you expect to stop when all I want is him to get back to me safe and sound. I don't care how long it takes as long as he promised to come back I'll wait.

AMANDA: How are you so sure that he will come back? For five years without fail you have written him a letter every month, have you ever received any single letter from him?

CALLIE: Cause he has promised and I trust him.

(Tamanna calling Amanda and Callie downstairs cause they received a letter)

TAMANNA: Look Callie! It's a letter.

(Callie excitedly open the letter)

HECTOR: Maybe the good Lord has answered our prayers.

(As Callie read the letter, the letter wasn't from Harold, it was from The General Baldwin)

TAMANNAANDAMANDA: What is it? You were so excited to open it, now what's with that face?

CALLIE: It's the letter from The General requesting Hector to join the army.

HECTOR: What!!?? Army!!?? No way can that be happening.

(All are shocked, as they are being noisy Patrick came to see what happened)

PATRICK: What's with all the sound and faces you made? What had happened inside this house?

AMANDA: We got the letter from The General Baldwin requesting Hector to join the army.

PATRICK: There's no way my beloved son is joining the army. I have lost my son-in-law Harold, there's no way I'm losing my son Hector. What if Hector hasn't come home for five years or what if we haven't received any information about him?

TAMANNA: But Papa, what can we do? It's a letter from The General. We just can't decline it, he'll be upset that he might even put us on probation.

PATRICK: Leave that to me. I'll take all the responsibilities. I can't take a risk and lose my son. I've lost your mom and Harold, there's no way I'm risking the life of my son. If necessary I'll be the one joining the army.

CALLIE: You gone mad Papa? Look at you, you're no longer in your 20s or 30s. You are getting older day by day, weaker day by day. Joining the army? Forget it. No one is joining the army. Whatever, we can't take a risk and lose Hector.

(All agrees and gets back to their work)

(As the night has come Callie couldn't sleep and think the whole night)

CALLIE: *(talking to herself)* Should I join the army and change myself as a male? And then my family will be safe. Maybe this is my answer to my prayers. A chance to see Harold and search for him there. For sure none is gonna agree with my decision so I have to do it secretly.

(The next day)

HECTOR: Good morning, sister.

CALLIE: Morning honey, how's dad?

HECTOR: He's still in his bed.

CALLIE: Great. *(Smiling)*

HECTOR: You look happy after such a long time.

CALLIE: Is it so?

HECTOR: Yea.

CALLIE: Look HECTOR, I want you to do me a favour.

HECTOR: Anything for you.

CALLIE: I plan on joining the army.

HECTOR: *(stunned and surprised)* Army!? Are you crazy? You are a woman!

CALLIE: I know, please Hector help me. Please.

(A minute of silence)

HECTOR: What is it?

CALLIE: Thank God. I want you to be a man and take responsibility and take care of Papa and his business and your two beloved sisters Amanda and Tamanna. I've taken care of you since you are born and I know you well and I know you are capable of looking after them. Please can you do that for me?

HECTOR: What about you?

CALLIE: You don't have to worry about that. You know me well too, right?

HECTOR: Yea

CALLIE: Good boy. Please help me out and I want you to keep this secret and don't tell Papa. Take good care of them for me as I always did to you. Take care of yourself too, don't ever skip your meals okay?

HECTOR: *(sobbing)* okay.

CALLIE: *(sobbing and smiling)* I love you and take care.

HECTOR: When are you going to leave?

CALLIE: By tomorrow's tonight

(As the night has come Callie cuts her hair off and leaves her house and joins the army.)

SCENE 5

(After Callie had finished training her army, she finally got the chance to stay where Harold had lived his life. Callie changed her name to Jack)

MAN 1: How is life here, Jack?

JACK: Good! All is well

MAN 1: That's good to hear. My life lately has been a mess.

JACK: No life can be perfect. We just have to accept and learn, my brother.

MAN 2: Hahaha...No worries, brother we all struggle everyday just to struggle for another day.

(All laughed)

MAN 1: So Jack, you haven't told me where you from? Are you married? Do you have a girlfriend?

JACK: Hahaha I better keep all those as a secret.

MAN 1: Okay I respect your words. Why not have drinks tonight?

(The night has come and Jack go to the bar with his new friends)

MAN 1: Hello beautiful ladies, get us three full cups of beer.

MAN 2: This is the best bar in town, Jack. I bet you haven't tasted any better beer than this.

JACK: Is it so? Let's see.

(They have their beer and are already drunk enough)

JACK: Gentlemen what a beautiful night it is, why not get ready to go.

MAN 2: One more please *(could barely speak)*

JACK: Gentleman please let me clock off. See you tomorrow. It's getting late.

(Jack left the bar and went home. Jack reached his house and his Pike is there to visit him)

PIKE: How are you Jack?

JACK: Am I getting too drunk or what? Look who I see?

PIKE: *(laughing)* Look at you my friend. Hahaha... Anyways, nice to see you again.

JACK: How did you enter? When did you come home? You've done your fishing.

PIKE: Yes done with fishing. I can now take a rest.

JACK: You still haven't answered me how you entered.

PIKE: Magic

JACK: Idiot

(Both chuckles)

JACK: You can stay here as long as you want.

PIKE: I feel so honoured to hear that.

(The next day Jack go out to buy food for both of them)

JACK: How much is the carrot?

(As he asked he saw Harold passing by and thought it as a mistake but follow him, as he follow he came to realise Harold is still alive and he's happy)

JACK:*(shouting)* Harold!!

(Harold turns back to see who called him)

HAROLD: Was it you who called me?

JACK: *(tearing up)* your voice is still like before.

HAROLD: Umm... Do I know you?

JACK: I hope so *(sobbing)*

HAROLD: Look, it's my first time seeing you. What's wrong? Have I done something wrong to you or your family? Why are you crying?

JACK: You Idiot! It's me *(sobbing)*

HAROLD: Me? Who?

JACK: *(barely speaking)* It's me. It's me, Callie. *(Crying)*

(Harold was stunned and unable to speak for a moment)

JACK: I thought you were dead. Where were you all that time? I've sent you so many letters, you haven't replied to any of them. Did you even read them?

HAROLD: What had happened to you? Are you sure you are Callie?

(Jack crying and Harold padding him)

(They both went to the nearby shop and had some tea, Jack came to realise that Harold had already started a new life and was married to his ex and their first child)

JACK: It hurt so good that I thought I had already tasted hell. But what can I do Harold? I wish you nothing but the best in your life. I hope you make your wife happy like you used to make me happy and safe. I wish to see your child as I failed to be the mother. Have a nice life, Harold.

HAROLD: For all those years I've sincerely loved you and you have filled my cups Callie. I'm ashamed that you see me like this that I have no guts to reply to all your letters. I've hurt you I know, please stop waiting for me and find another person who is worth waiting for. I wish you all the best foe that.

(Jack reach his home and Pike patiently waiting for him)

PIKE: Welcome back, Jack.

JACK: Wow what's this? You've prepared us dinner?

PIKE: Why not, letting me stay here is already a blessing for me.

JACK: Stop saying that you've helped all those times when I was in need. So this is my duty and responsibility, Pike.

PIKE: *(laughing)* Let's eat before it gets cold. I've got a special wine for tonight too.

JACK: Great! Sure

PIKE: So where have you been all day? You came home so late?

JACK: I passed by my old friend and we had our talks, that's it.

PIKE: I see. (The night getting darker and both were getting drunk)

PIKE: Come, you're drunk now. I'll put you to sleep, Callie.

CALLIE: *(was shocked)* Callie? How did you know me?

PIKE: I'm sorry I didn't mean to call you like that.

CALLIE: How did you know my name? Answer me please.

PIKE: I've already known that you are a woman ever since I took care of you when you were sick. And then I asked one of my friends to know who you really are. I'm so sorry Callie for not telling you. I thought of not standing in your way, that's why I kept my silence.

CALLIE: You better have told me earlier, Pike.

PIKE: I'm sorry Callie, I try my best to see you as a friend but I keep on falling deeper every time I see you. I'm sorry Callie. I'm truly sorry.

CALLIE: Let's talk tomorrow. We are drunk now. Good night.

PIKE: Good night, Callie.

(After half a year of being in a relationship Pike and Callie finally decided to marry)

PIKE: I can't wait to introduce you in front of my family. I've kept telling and sending them letters about you. My mom is eager to see you.

CALLIE: I'm happy to hear that Pike. I finally feel alive again. My dad is getting weaker day by day, I can't stop thinking of him. He really wants to see you Pike.

(As they introduced to both their families after few month they had married)

PIKE: I never imagined I would wake up next to an angel.

CALLIE: *(smile)* Morning Honey.

PIKE: Morning my dear.

(Callie finally married her lover and finally felt alive again. After one year of marriage they gave Birth to their first child)

PIKE: Hello, my sweet little baby. Mommy will be right back *(kiss on the forehead of his child)*

CALLIE: How's the baby?

PIKE: Just like the father, good as always.

CALLIE: Come to Mama, my baby. Let me feed you.

PIKE: I need to go fishing again tomorrow.

CALLIE: Arghh!! Again!!?? Can't you just take leave only for this week? How many times have they assigned you? It pissed me off.

PIKE: Look who's getting angry *(smile)* Don't worry, this will be the last I promise. After this I'll surely spare my time for you and our child. Happy? Hmm?

CALLIE: Fine. Don't break that promise.

PIKE: Sure honey.

(The next day has come and Pike went for fishing, everything was fine until Pike's friend came to tell Callie what had happened)

MAN: *(rushing)* Is anyone home!?

CALLIE: What is it?

MAN: Mrs. Callie I've come to tell you that the beat where Pike and his friends went for fishing has sunk and no bodies have been found.

CALLIE: What are you saying! Nonsense! Please tell me it's not true. Please tell me if you have mistaken the boat. Tell me my Pike is still there. Tell me please!!

(Callie crying)

(As three days have passed and no bodies have been found they all thought that the fishermen including Pike had died. They had given up and were preparing to have a funeral for them. Pike's funeral)

CALLIE: This is how it starts and how it ends. I saw you in my dream but never realised that man was you PIKE. Can we change and start from the beginning? I'm still not ready for this Honey.

(Harold also attend the funeral and approach Callie)

HAROLD: *(padding Callie)* It's okay to cry out your heart like you did before. My chest and shoulders are always there. Cry, cry, cry until you have had enough.

(After half an hour of the funeral Harold and Callie had their talking)

CALLIE: Thank you for coming

HAROLD: You don't have to thank me. It's what I'm supposed to do.

CALLIE: Still though, I'm touched by your presence here.

HAROLD: I came to answer your question.

CALLIE: What question?

HAROLD: Yes I've read all the letters you've sent without skipping any of them. I've read them all. I was a coward, Callie. Every Time the postman came there's not a single day I wasn't happy but I was a coward to send you back a letter because I was still in love with Judy. I apologise for that and I will never be forgiven. Until then, stay strong and healthy. Now you've already become a mother and I know you are brave and wise, so I wish you all the best. Your child is the luckiest child to have a mother like you and a hardworking father like Pike, as I failed to be the father of your child.

(Exeunt)

X

KNITTING QUALM - JOSHUA B

SCENE - 1

SANTIAGO: Where's she? They're waiting for her.

SNEHA: Ahem! Love I tried calling all her friends but she doesn't seem to answer the phone

SANTIAGO: This is all your fault. I kept warning you about the company she loafed with!

SNEHA: You think this is my fault!? Where's all the love you pampered her with??

Don't you blame it on me.

SANTIAGO: You wretch! Don't raise your voice (*Slaps her*)

(The bridegroom family enters the kitchen hurriedly)

SHEKHAR: Is everything alright Sneha? Where's Rihanna?

Santiago, why are you shouting at your wife?

SANTIAGO: Ah the women in my family are going to bring shame on my reputation.

SNEHA: You and your wretched fame, are you humiliating me and our daughter in front of our guests??

MRS.SHEKAR: Oh both of you stop this.

SNEHA: He's the one who has to.

SANTIAGO: ME? You adulteress, you brought that onto yourself.

SHEKHAR: That's enough Santiago, stop ill-treating your wife.

SANTIAGO: She's a harlot.

The entire Mr.Shekhar's family exclaims "Oh good lord"

SNEHA: *(Crying)* What have I not sacrificed for this family? Haven't I loved you enough Santu? I let you use my body for you to quench your thirst. *(Sobbing)*

You have never learnt to respect me, but you've loved all the things that I haven't done.

SANTIAGO: You snake! Don't you blasphemy

You go to parties with different men from your work and you let me quench my thirst?

MRS.SHEKHAR: I think we'll take leave *(Hesitating)*

SANTIAGO: Yes please and save your son from my wretched daughter who resembles her mother.

(Sneha crying hard runs into the room)

SANTIAGO: There she runs away, her old slithering witty charm

SHEKHAR: All right then, call us when Rihanna shows up

SANTIAGO: That snake will be sleeping with men like her mother

Quit her! Mr.Shekhar

(Mr. Shekhar's family walks out with dismay)

(Santiago walks into the mini bar, picks up a whiskey and sits on his favourite rocky chair near the fire)

SCENE - 2

(Rihanna driving fast with her friends)

1ST FRIEND: Hey your mom has been calling you for a very long time, don't you think you should answer her

(Rihanna increases the volume)

2ND FRIEND: Rihanna! Rihanna!!! Can you stop the stupid music?

RIHANNA: What's your problem girls?? I escape reality and come here to be with you. And you don't even understand it.

1ST FRIEND: Alright calm down

(Rihanna increases the speed of the car)

1 & 2 FRIENDS: Talk to us Rihanna. What's happening to you??

RIHANNA: Quit it ladies, I'm not interested to even talk about it

1ST FRIEND: Alright alright.

(Rihanna burst out crying)

RIHANNA: They doubt me for everything, my dad thinks I loaf around selling my body to the men out there. He's forcing me to get married, while I wanna live an independent life of my own. A life I cherish, a life I love.

2ND FRIEND: What about your mother??

RIHANNA: Her voice is never heard, she is shun down every time she tries helping me. She's physically and mentally abused by my father. Do I need men to live my life?? Why does he doubt his own daughter?

1ST FRIEND: Don't cry Rihu, it's alright, dads being dads. We know how much you respect yourself, you do not have to cry about it

RIHANNA: I escaped home because my dad's friend's son likes me, he had asked for my hand.

He's a nice guy but I don't think I wanna be married any sooner.

(Phone rings again)

RIHANNA: (picks it up and shouts)What's with your calling ma?? Why are you torturing me?

(Sneha cries over the phone)

RIHANNA: Mama talk to me ...

(Sneha continues crying and Rihanna hears a thud)

RIHANNA: Mummy! Ma can you please talk??? Where are you? What happened to you?

(Rihanna starts getting scared; 1&2 friend's starts panicking takes the phone from Rihanna)

1ST FRIEND: Aunty, Aunty it's Karishma here. Are you alright aunty? Hello? Hello?

SCENE - 3

(Shekhar enters his house kitchen)

SHEKHAR: What's wrong with Mr. Santiago's family, why are they acting strange?

JACOB: Dada, Rihanna doesn't seem interested in the marriage, maybe that's the issue

SHEKHAR: No, her dad was the one who asked for you to marry her

JACOB: Me?? Why me?

SHEKHAR: I don't know he is always very fond of you

JACOB: Okayy that's so strange

SHEKHAR: Tell me Jacob, do you like her??

JACOB: Dad she's really pretty and kind, YES! I like her but does she like me?? That's the real question because I don't wanna spend my married days with someone who feels forced

SHEKHAR: Maybe she'll fall in love with eventually like your mother did *(smiling)*

But their family is the one that I fear. They seem so too spicy for a family like ours. I don't like the way he disrespected the women in his house.

JACOB: Dada let's not gossip about them. What if they start talking or finding fault within us?

SHEKHAR: Alright my son, I was just being mindful

SCENE - 4

(Friend 1 & Friend 2 at the tea shop)

1ST FRIEND: Why's Rihanna dad that way?

2ND FRIEND: What do you mean Margret?

1ST FRIEND: I mean, he's torturing them so much and they do not deserve it

2ND FRIEND: It's because he's not the biological dad of Rihanna, and that's why doesn't have a connection with her.

1ST FRIEND: WHAT HE'S NOT HER BIOLOGICAL DAD?

2ND FRIEND: Biological dad! He's her step dad.

1ST FRIEND: What happened to her real father? Is he alive? Why did her mother marry Santiago then?

2ND FRIEND: Oh stop it will you!! I do not have answers for everything you ask. Let's go to Rihanna's house and she might answer your questions.

1ST FRIEND: Yes she may need mental support. I wonder what happened to her mom, Rihu left so worried

SCENE - 5

SANTIAGO: Hey Sneha! Stop whining and get me some soup. I'm very hungry. (No sign of Sneha)

Sneha! Sneha! (Starts reading newspaper, and forgets about Sneha)

(Rihanna runs inside the house hurriedly)

RIHANNA: Mummy mummy?? Where are you?

SANTIAGO: Here comes the princess(wakes up in anger and slaps her)

RIHANNA: Why's mum crying?

SANTIAGO: You fool around the town lying beside men and how are you walking into my house. It was a shame to see Mr.Shekhar wait for a wretched fool like you.

RIHANNA: Can you stop it dad! (*Shouts*) I wanna see mummy!

SANTIAGO: Let that cheater rot to death (Rihanna tries to hit dad)don't you call her that

She's been so loyal to you and all you've done is doubt both mum and me. You've always shamed us because you're insecure and do not trust us. What have we done to deserve this? Why don't you trust us a little? Have we ever disrespected you while you abused us? All we ever want is for you to trust us and help us because you're the man of the house .I've never wanted to tell you this but I do really hate you! (Dad walks away with shame)

RIHANNA: *(shouting)* We do not deserve this life dad, you're the trauma dad *(crying loudly)*

(Exeunt)

XI

FATE'S BATTLEFIELD: LOVE AMONGST RIVALRY - LEKITHA D S

(Setting: A grand banquet hall enhanced with luxurious tapestries, each bearing the emblem of one of two different noble families, the Montilii and the Valerii. A splendid banquet is in full swing, with nobles and servants enthusiastic about.)

SCENE 1

(The focus on Coriolanus and warrior)

CORIOLANUS: (In a hushed tone to a fellow Montilii warrior) Who is she? In the middle of this throng, she exudes an aura of gentleness that seems to make the air itself gentler.

MONTILII WARRIOR: (Whispering back) that's Virgilia Valerii, a dove among predators, all say. Be careful, Coriolanus. Our families have been rivals throughout many eras.

(Despite the warning, Coriolanus continues to move smoothly through the crowd, all the while keeping his eyes fixed on Virgilia.)

CORIOLANUS:(With politeness, as he draws near to Virgilia) Lady Virgilia, tonight, fate has crafted an unexpected twist. I am Coriolanus of the Montilii, and I have never been more mesmerised.

VIRGILIA: (*Blushing, a hint of a smile*) Coriolanus, your renown as a formidable warrior is widely acknowledged, however, your tenderness catches me off guard.

(While conversing, they realise a mutual love for art, culture, and a yearning for a world liberated from the confines of their warring families. The tension in the room between the Montilii and the Valerii only intensifies their bond. The SCENE concludes with Coriolanus and Virgilia lingering gazes, suggesting the budding attraction that defies their families' long standing rivalry.)

SCENE 2

(The moonlight casts a silver sheen over a hidden garden, secluded from prying eyes. Coriolanus and Virgilia stand beneath a trellis adorned with aromatic roses, their Fingers interlocked, their love a fragile secret. Coriolanus and Virgilia had started to meet secretly and both fell in love and confessed to each other)

VIRGILIA: (In a hushed tone, her voice trembled with a blend of excitement and anxiety)Coriolanus, this forbidden love, it kindles an intense flame inside me, yet I shudder at the risk it brings.

CORIOLANUS: (His voice overflowing with zeal and unwavering commitment) Virgilia, my heart has made its decision, and it has chosen you. We shall face this storm together, no matter how fierce it may become.

(Their love deepens in this hidden sanctuary, far from the judgmental eyes of their feuding families. The scent of roses surrounds them as they speak of their devotion.)

VIRGILIA: (Her gaze fixed on Coriolanus) My love, the animosity between our families threatens to separate us?Can we truly withstand the forces that conspire against us?

CORIOLANUS: (His gaze fixed on Virgilia's face) Virgilia, love knows no boundaries, and I would confront any obstacle to be by your side. Our love, like the deepest roots, will endure.

(They cherish stolen moments, whispered vows, and savour lingering touches, all in the face of growing challenges and sacrifices. Their love deepens with each passing day.)

VIRGILIA: (Tears glistening in her eyes)Coriolanus, My heart pains as we must make sacrifices to conceal our love. But I would rather have but a moment with you than an eternity without.

CORIOLANUS: (His thumb gently brushing away her tears) Virgilia, our love is an unquenchable fire that persists, even in the darkest of times, we shall endure, for love, like us, love is unwavering.

(As the days turn into weeks, and the weeks into months, their forbidden love story becomes more complicated.)

VIRGILIA: (Speaking softly to each other while they hold each other close beneath a trellis adorned with aromatic roses) Coriolanus, the danger of being found out increases every time we steal these moments. How can we navigate these precarious circumstances?

CORIOLANUS: (Holding her close, his voice unyielding) We must proceed with caution, Virgilia. Our love is our most precious possession, and we will protect it at all costs.

(Their love story becomes a careful juggling act, a balance between their yearning for each other and the ever-present threat of their families' discovery.)

VIRGILIA: (As they part, a sense of longing in her eyes) Coriolanus, assure me that regardless of the challenges we face, we will stand strong together.

CORIOLANUS: (His fingers tracing her cheek) I promise, Virgilia. Our love is a guiding light in the blackest of nights, guiding us through the difficulty.

(Despite the mounting challenges and the constant threat of discovery, their love continues to deepen with each stolen moment. Their forbidden love story evolves into a testament of unwavering devotion and the enduring power of love.)

SCENE 3

(The SCENE unfolds in a dimly lit chamber within Coriolanus's family estate, where shadows loom like ominous spectres. Coriolanus, a once-vigorous warrior, stands alone, his countenance marred by anguish. The contents of the letter, a looming threat to his cherished love, cast a pall of anguish upon his once-vigorous countenance.)

CORIOLANUS: (His voice, laden with despair)What have I done?

(Rivals of Coriolanus, were aware of his unconditional love for Virgilia, took advantage of his weakness or used his vulnerability to their advantage. Virgilia, stands alone in the garden of her family's estate, bathed in the ethereal glow of the moonlight. Tears stream down her face as she clutches a crumpled letter, its words a venomous betrayal that tears her heart.)

VIRGILIA: *(Whispering through her tears)* How could you do it Coriolanus?

(As their love falls apart due to the burden of betrayal, a divide widens between Coriolanus and Virgilia, each struggling to come to terms with the gravity of the situation.)

CORIOLANUS: Facing his enemies, his voice quivering with regret, I did it to protect her, but the cost is too high. My heart aches with regret.

VIRGILIA: *(Her voice quivering, with a heart heavy of sorrow)* Our love was our sanctuary, Coriolanus, but now it feels like a prison.

(Even amidst the great divide, a longing for reconciliation and redemption simmers beneath the surface.)

CORIOLANUS: (Touched by the guiltiness of his actions, he asks forgiveness) Virgilia, I did it to protect you from their Deceptive and manipulative political tactics, but now I see I've brought you more problems and pain.

(Virgilia, though hurt, yearns for the return of the love that always warmed her heart.)

VIRGILIA: (with a displaying a sense of openness and a deep yearning) Coriolanus, I know now that your love was genuine and never doubtful. Is it possible for us to rediscover our connection?

(Through forgiveness and understanding, they backtrack on a journey to heal the wounds inflicted by betrayal.)

CORIOLANUS: (*Determined*) Virgilia, I'm willing to do whatever is necessary to demonstrate my love and regain your trust.

VIRGILIA: (With a small ray of hope.) Coriolanus, let's confront our families together, show them the strength of our love, and create a future where it prevails over betrayal.

(As they stand together in the face of hardships, their love becomes a testament to resilience and the power of redemption. The SCENE shifts to a moonlit night, the garden bathed in silvery luminescence. Coriolanus and Virgilia, facing each other, their expressions a mix of sorrow, longing, and hope, stand at the heart of the garden, surrounded by blooming roses.)

CORIOLANUS: (*His voice filled with determination*) Virgilia, I have betrayed not only you but I've let down our love deeply. But I swear now, I will do whatever it takes to make compensation.

VIRGILIA: (Her eyes filled with tears, But with a small ray of hope for forgiveness.) Coriolanus, our love has faced many problems, but it has not been extinguished. Can we find our way back together, despite the darkness that surrounds us?

CORIOLANUS: (Approaching Virgilia, his hand stretched in front, seeking to come together.) Let us rebuild what we once had, stronger and more resilient than before. Together, we can face our families and the tempest that brews in their hearts.

(Virgilia, her heart broken between the pain of betrayal and the hope of redemption, hesitates for a moment before placing her trembling hand in Coriolanus's.)

VIRGILIA: *(With a trembling smile)* Coriolanus, I believe in our love. Let us prove that it can withstand any problem and circumstances, even betrayal.

(Their hands interlocked, Coriolanus and Virgilia step forward, determined to face their families and the challenges that lie ahead.)

CORIOLANUS: *(His voice resolute)* Together, Virgilia, we shall stand above this betrayal, and our love shall shine in the darkest of times.

(As they venture into the unknown, their love story becomes a powerful testament to the enduring strength of love, redemption, and the resilience of the human heart.)

SCENE 4:

(The scene opens in a beautifully adorned garden, now bathed in the warm light of the morning sun. Roses bloom in vibrant colours, symbolising the renewal of love. Coriolanus and Virgilia stand at the heart of the garden, their hands tightly entwined, their eyes reflecting the depth of their affection.)

CORIOLANUS: *(His voice brimming with gratitude and love)* Virgilia, our journey has been with many problems and ups and down, but here we stand, successfully.

VIRGILIA: *(With a beautiful smile adorned)* Coriolanus, our love has faced the toughest challenges and come out even more resilient and united. There is nothing we cannot overcome together.

(As they embrace, their families, the Montilii and the Valerii, enter the garden. The air is filled with anticipation and uncertainty.)

MONTILLI PATRIARCH: (looking at Coriolanus, his voice in curiosity) Coriolanus, what is the meaning of this gathering? Why have you gathered us here?

VALERII MATRIARCH: (Looking at Virgilia, her expression cautious) Yes, and why is Virgilia here with the Montilii?

(Coriolanus and Virgilia stepped forward, hand in hand.)

CORIOLANUS: *(With genuineness)* Noble families, we present ourselves not as representatives of the Montilii and Valerii clans, but as Coriolanus and Virgilia, two individuals whose love rises above the conflicts between our noble houses.

VIRGILIA: *(With unwavering determination in her tone.)* We have chosen love over hatred, unity over division, and today, we invite you to do the same.

(The families exchange confused looks, yet there's an unmistakable feeling of potential and hope in the atmosphere.)

MONTILLI PATRIARCH: *(thoughtful)* Coriolanus, I have seen the change in you, the depth of your love for Virgilia. Could it be that love has the power to heal our wounds?

VALERII MATRIARCH: *(Her heart softened by Virgilia's happiness)* And Virgilia, you look dazzling beside Coriolanus. Therefore it's time for us to put aside our pride and anger.

(Coriolanus and Virgilia take a step closer to each other, their love a shining example.)

CORIOLANUS: *(With hope)* Families, our love has shown us a path beyond rivalry. Let us put aside our pride and honour, and embrace the power of unity.

VIRGILIA: (interlocking hands with Coriolanus) Together, we can build a future where love triumphs over conflict.

(The Montilii and Valerii, deeply moved by the sincerity of Coriolanus and Virgilia, begin to lower their guard. Slowly, family members from both sides approach, extending greetings.)

MONTILLI PATRIARCH: (Addressing the assembly) Let this day mark a new beginning. A beginning where the Montilii and the Valerii stand united, for the sake of love and peace.

VALERII MATRIARCH: (Nodding) Let our families join together, just as Coriolanus and Virgilia's hearts are entwined.

(Amidst the applause and cheers, the Montilii and Valerii families shake hands and embrace, setting aside decades of rivalry.)

CORIOLANUS: *(Whispering to Virgilia)* our love has not only brought us back but also brought redemption to our family and world.

VIRGILIA: *(Smiling)* Love possesses the remarkable power to mend the most profound of scars.

(The SCENE transitions to a joyous celebration in the garden. Tables are laden with sumptuous feasts, and laughter fills the air. Coriolanus and Virgilia, now united, exchange vows of eternal love.)

CORIOLANUS: *(His voice filled with unwavering devotion)* Virgilia, I vow to cherish and protect our love, to be your unwavering support through all the life.

VIRGILIA: *(Her eyes sparkling with love and affection)* Coriolanus, I vow to stand by your side, to be your partner and confidante, to face whatever challenges come our way with the strength of our love.

(As they exchange rings, their families look on with tears of joy. The celebration continues late into the night, a testament to the newfound harmony between the Montilii and the Valerii.)

VIRGILIA: (As they dance beneath the stars) Coriolanus, our love has no limits, and our families are united. We have found our happily ever after.

CORIOLANUS: *(Whispering in Virgilia's ear)* And so, my love, our story, once marked by conflict and betrayal, has become a tale of redemption and enduring love.

(As Coriolanus and Virgilia continue to dance, their love shines like a beacon, lighting up the night and guiding the way for all who witness their powerful journey.)

(Exits)

XII
THE WEIGHT OF WAR - PALLAVI RANI

ACT 1

(The play opens in the royal council chamber of King Henry V. King Henry sits at the head of the council table, flanked by his trusted advisor, Sir Thomas Erpingham, and his military officer, Captain Fluellen. The council members are gathered to discuss the ongoing war with France.)

KING HENRY: (addressing the council) My lords and advisors, the war with France continues to weigh heavily on my conscience. We have seen too much bloodshed, and our soldiers bear the burdens of battle.

SIR THOMASERPINGHAM: (nods) Indeed, Your Majesty. The toll of this war is great, not only in lives lost but in the suffering of our people.

CAPTAINFLUELLEN: (saluting) Your Majesty, our troops are valiant, but they grow weary. We've captured Harfleur, but our march through France is perilous.

DUKE OF BEDFORD: (concerned) Your Majesty, we must consider the cost of this war. Our treasury is strained, and our people suffer.

DUKE OF EXETER: (supporting the king) But, Your Majesty, we have a claim to the French throne, and we cannot simply abandon it.

KING HENRY: (*pauses*) I am mindful of the suffering, and it troubles my soul. Yet, we cannot simply abandon our campaign. Our claim to the French throne remains, and the war must be resolved.

(The council members exchange concerned glances.)

(The following SCENE takes place in a private chamber where King Henry V and Sir Thomas Erpingham receive a message from Princess Katherine of France, who has been negotiating with the French court.)

PRINCESS KATHERINE: (enter, holding a sealed letter) Your Majesty, I bring news from the French court. They have expressed a desire for peace and propose a truce.

SIR THOMAS ERPINGHAM: (*curious*) A truce, Your Highness?

KING HENRY: (takes the letter) Let me see it. (Reads) They offer a truce, during which we will cease hostilities, and negotiations for a lasting peace will begin.

(King Henry ponders the letter.)

(The next SCENE unfolds in the council chamber, where the council members passionately debate the merits of the proposed truce.)

DUKE OF BEDFORD: (*urgently*) Your Majesty, we must consider the truce. Our soldiers are fatigued, and our treasury strained.

DUKE OF EXETER: (*opposing*) But what of our claim to the French throne? We cannot simply abandon it!

DUKE OF YORK: (*supporting the truce*) Your Majesty, the people are weary of war. A truce would bring relief and hope for a lasting peace.

NYM: (entering, with a humorous tone) Your Majesty, May I suggest a feast to celebrate this truce? The men could use a good meal!

(The council members exchange heated arguments and differing views.)

KING HENRY: (*rising*) Enough! I must make a decision. (*Pauses*) Call for a meeting with the French envoy. We will explore the terms of this truce.

(The council members, though divided, nod in agreement.)

(In this symbolic scene, Satan, representing the temptation of war, appears to King Henry V in a dream.)

SATAN: (*whispers*) Do not waver, King Henry. The glory of conquest awaits you. Continue the war, and you shall be immortalised.

(King Henry struggles with his decision as he battles the temptation represented by Satan.)

KING HENRY: (*in turmoil*) No! The cost is too great. I must seek a path to peace.

(The play concludes in the council chamber, where King Henry V announces his decision regarding the truce.)

KING HENRY: (addressing the council) I have met with the French envoy. We shall accept the truce and engage in negotiations for lasting peace.

(The council members react with a mix of relief and concern.)

SIR THOMAS ERPINGHAM: (*approving*) Your wisdom prevails, Your Majesty.

CAPTAIN FLUELLEN: (*saluting*) It is a path to a more honourable peace.

PRINCESS KATHERINE: (*entering*) Your Majesty, your decision brings hope for an end to this long and bitter conflict.

(King Henry's decisive choice brings hope for an end to the war and sets the stage for diplomatic negotiations. The council members, though divided, acknowledge the need for peace.)

XIII

SOLACE IN THE FOREST OF ARDEN - SMITI LEPCHA

SCENE 1

(Enter Duke Senior, Oliver. The SCENE is set in Duke Senior's palace)

DUKE SENIOR: What brings you here, Oliver?

OLIVER: I am here to have a word with you sir.

DUKE SENIOR: What is it?

OLIVER: It's about Rosalind, my lord. I have some concerns.

DUKE: Rosalind? What bothers you about her?

OLIVER: Well, my lord, I've been observing her closely, and I fear that it may not be the right to keep her in the court anymore.

DUKE SENIOR: Go on. What makes you think that?

OLIVER: Rosalind, my lord, she's quite headstrong and independent. One of my men had spotted her and my brother Orlando after the wrestling match together. They were seen conversing in loving words for each other. If what he said is true this can cause a huge threat to your throne and my pride as their marriage could lead my brother to be the duke. My hate rate for my brother still remains and I can't let that happens

DUKE SENIOR: I see where you are coming from

.

OLIVER: The consequences of her intelligence and spirit, my lord. by removing them, you could preserve your throne.

DUKE SENIOR: Very well, Oliver. Your concern is valid. I will banish Rosalind from the court and you order a secret assignation of Orlando and Rosalind.

(Oliver and Duke Senior exit)

SCENE 2

(Enter Rosalind, Celia and touchstone in the forest of Arden.)

ROSALIND: Celia, I can hardly believe I am kicked out from the court and we are forced to flee to the Forest of Arden.

CELIA: Rosalind, we are in a difficult situation but we are in this together. That's what matters most. Besides, I'd rather be here with you than back in that oppressive court.

ROSALIND: Now that is true. You are always there to cheer me up. You always know how to bring comfort, my dear cousin.

CELIA: And don't forget Touch stone is here with us.

TOUCHSTONE: Indeed, girls. I may not be a forest expert, but I do have a knack for making people laugh. Laughter can be a powerful weapon in tough times.

ROSALIND: I suppose we'll need all the humour we can get in these unfamiliar surroundings.

CELIA: It may be different from what we are used to but it has its own beauty. The air is fresher, the trees are greener, and there's a certain peace here that we couldn't find at home.

ROSALIND: You're right, Celia. Perhaps this exile is a blessing in disguise. It gives me a chance to find myself.

CELIA: And I'll be right by your side, Rosalind, every step of the way.

TOUCHSTONE: And I'll be here to provide you guys with some jokes.

ROSALIND: Thank you, both of you. Let's embrace this new adventure and see where it takes us. Who knows what we'll discover about ourselves and the world in the Forest of Arden?

(Rosalind Celia and touchstone exits)

SCENE 3

ROSALIND (AS GANYMEDE): Well, Celia, it seems our decision to take on new identities was a wise one. As Ganymede, I can move about freely without arousing suspicion.

CELIA (AS ALIENA): Yes, Rosalind, and as Aliena, I can accompany you as your sister, which will help maintain our cover. But I must admit, it's strange to be living like this.

ROSALIND (AS GANYMEDE): It is, indeed. But think of it as an adventure, dear cousin. We get to explore life from a different perspective. And I have a feeling that our time in the Forest of Arden will teach us much about the world and ourselves.

(Several forest dwellers enter with Orlando)

FOREST DWELLER 1: stop there, travellers. How dare you venture into our forest?

ROSALIND (AS GANYMEDE): We don't mean any harm. We only seek refuge and solace in these woods.

CELIA (AS ALIENA): Yes, we are just travellers, looking for a quiet place to live our lives away from the world's troubles.

FOREST DWELLER 2: You look like you are from the court, and yet you claim to seek solace in our home. We don't trust you.

ROSALIND (AS GANYMEDE): We may have come from the court, but we are tired of its ways. We wish to embrace the simplicity of nature and live harmoniously with the forest.

CELIA (AS ALIENA): Please, we mean no harm to your home. We only ask for your guidance and acceptance.

FOREST DWELLER 3: You don't seem to be lying, and your intentions seem sincere. Very well, travellers. You may pass. But remember, the Forest of Arden is a testing ground. It will reveal your true selves in no time

ROSALIND (AS GANYMEDE): Thank you, kind dwellers, for understanding. We will honour this forest and live in harmony.

FOREST DWELLER 3: You, young traveller, carry a hidden burden.

ROSALIND (AS GANYMEDE): I may carry secrets, like any of us do. But for now I only seek solace and enlightenment in this forest.

FOREST DWELLER 3: Solace and enlightenment, two noble pursuits indeed. But tell me, what is the nature of the burden you bear, and why have you come to the Forest of Arden to lay it down?

ROSALIND (AS GANYMEDE): My burden is of love. I have come to this forest to understand the depths of my own heart, to discover whether my love true and enduring

FOREST DWELLER 3: You seek answers in this forest, but remember, the truth often lies within, waiting to be uncovered.

ROSALIND (AS GANYMEDE): Wise one, do you suggest that the answers to my heart's desires are within me, waiting to be revealed?

FOREST DWELLER 3: Indeed, young traveller. Here, the heart speaks its truth. But be prepared, for the journey it can be very tiring.

ROSALIND (AS GANYMEDE):*(Determined)* I am ready to face the challenges of this forest, both internal and external. I will search my heart and uncover the truth, whatever it may be.

PROFOUND FOREST DWELLER: *(Bowing slightly)* Then may the forest guide your steps, and may your heart find the answers it seeks. The journey has just begun, and the path ahead is filled with mystery.

(Enter Orlando)

ORLANDO:(to Rosalind)What brings you to this wilderness young man?

ROSALIND (AS GANYMEDE): Ah, good sir, I am a fellow traveller in search of solace and contemplation. The forest offers a solace from the troubles of the court.

ORLANDO: I couldn't agree more. This place is far removed from the demands of courtly life.

ROSALIND (AS GANYMEDE): And what brings you to the Forest of Arden, sir? You seem to have adapted well to this new way of life.

ORLANDO: I am escaping my brother. I have found freedom and security here So, I left everything behind.

ROSALIND (AS GANYMEDE): I, too, am here to explore the beauty and serenity of this forest, to discover the truths of life and love.

ORLANDO: Ah, love... it can be both a source of joy and torment. Love has brought challenges to me as well. But here in the forest, I hope to find clarity.

ROSALIND (AS GANYMEDE): The forest has a way of revealing the truths we often hide from ourselves. I wish you the best on your journey, Orlando. May you find the answers your heart desires.

(They exit)

SCENE 4

(Enter Orlando and Rosalind walking through the forest)

ROSALIND (AS GANYMEDE): Orlando, I have an unconventional idea. To help you win your lover's heart, why don't we stage a playful role-play, right here in the heart of the forest?

ORLANDO: A role-play, Ganymede? How would that work?

ROSALIND (AS GANYMEDE): Imagine this, Orlando. I will momentarily become Rosalind, and you will be yourself. We'll enact a SCENE as if we were meeting after a long time and you can practise your wooing.

ORLANDO: How should I approach her? What should I say?

ROSALIND (AS GANYMEDE): Orlando, love is a delicate dance. Be sincere and speak from the heart. Tell her about her beauty, her wit, and the way she makes you feel.

ORLANDO: oh, my Rosalind, there's something I've been meaning to tell you, something that has been burning in my heart since I first laid eyes on you.

ROSALIND (AS GANYMEDE): What is it, Orlando?

ORLANDO: It's difficult to find the right words, but here it is: Ganymede, my heart belongs to you, and it has since the moment I saw you. Your eyes, your smile, your laughter—they all captivate me in a way I can't describe.

ROSALIND (AS GANYMEDE): Oh, Orlando! You take me by surprise.

ORLANDO: It's true, Ganymede. Every thought, every breath is filled with you. You've become the centre of my world.

ROSALIND (AS GANYMEDE): Orlando, your words are like music to my ears. (Exit Rosalind, Celia and Orlando)

SCENE 5

(Enter Oliver in the forest of Arden)

OLIVER: What is this place? I feel uneasy here.

This forest is not like any other forest. It looks mystical. (Enter a forest dweller)

FOREST DWELLER: another one from the courts. Are you one with the people before, or is the way of the court too much for those attending there?

OLIVER: the people before? (Aside) so Orlando and Rosalind are here.

FOREST DWELLER: Oliver, I sense a heavy burden in your heart.

OLIVER: How do you know my name, and who are you? (The surrounding turns more mystical)

FOREST DWELLER: *(in an enchanting voice)* Names are not important here. What matters is the pain that weighs you down. I sense a rift between you and your brother, Orlando.

OLIVER:(in a trance) Yes, you're right. I've treated him terribly.

FOREST DWELLER: The forest has a way of revealing the truth in one's heart. But it also offers a chance for redemption. Seek out Orlando, mend the bonds that have been broken, and find peace within yourself.

OLIVER: I will. Thank you for showing me the way.

(Exit Oliver running like a mad man. The forest dweller disappears; Enter Rosalind[as Ganymede] Orlando and Celia[as Aliena])

ROSALIND (AS GANYMEDE): You look really sad, tell me what troubles you.

ORLANDO: my heart feels heavy as it feels like a century since I last saw Rosalind.

She's unlike anyone I've ever met. Her wit, her charm, her laughter – they all enchant me.

ROSALIND: oh, my poor soul (Revealing her true identity) Orlando, it's me, Rosalind! I've been disguised as Ganymede all this time.

ORLANDO: Rosalind? Is the forest playing tricks on me? Oh! If it is the magic of the forest then I don't want it to stop.

CELIA: it is no magic. She speaks the truth. As I am Celia. I've been by your side, testing your love and you have proven fit for my lovely Rosalind.

(Enter Oliver)

ORLANDO: oh, my cruel brother. Have you come here to end my life? I won't let that happen as I am the happiest now.

OLIVER: No, the forest has shown me the right path. I want to mend things with you. I discovered that my hatred for you just makes me a terrible person.

CELIA: That sounds wonderful. This forest is truly a mystical place. There is something I need to confess.

ROSALIND: What is it, Celia?

CELIA: These past few weeks, I have come to realise something. Something that I can no longer keep to myself.

OLIVER: Please, go on.

CELIA: I've fallen in love with you, Oliver. I never expected it, but my heart has found its way to you.

OLIVER: Celia, I can't express how happy that makes me. I've been feeling the same way about you.

ROSALIND: Let's put an end to these mistaken identities and have a double wedding, Orlando.

CELIA: Yes, a double wedding sounds perfect.

(They exit)

XIV
THE QUEST FOR LOVE AND REDEMPTION - SHUBASHREE SABAT

SCENE 1

(Antioch, a room in the Palace, enter Antiochus, Prince of Tyre and his subjects)

ANTIOCHUS: Pleasure to have you, The Prince of Tyre! Hope you're aware of your next move.

PERICLES: I am Antiochus. Fear of death is disgraceful for a glorified Prince.

ANTIOCHUS: Bring in our beautiful daughter who's going to be a bride.

(Enters Antiochus' daughter)

PERICLES: (seeing her astonishingly)What a Beauty! As if spring has arrived, she is reminding me of all the poetries I've read. She is as graceful as the complete moon, anyone would die in love.

ANTIOCHUS: (*angrily*) Prince Pericles! Watch your words. She's the Princess of Antioch.

PERICLES: (*smilingly; to Antiochus' daughter*) I'm burning in love of yours, where life or death doesn't matter but you.

ANTIOCHUS: An advice for you Prince,

Solve the riddle to wed my daughter. If you fail, so will your head. Read the conclusion before you bleed.

DAUGHTER: I wish all happiness, may your actions prove your words.

The Riddle

'I am no viper, but I fed on my mother's flesh, which caused me to reproduce;

I sought a husband, in which I laboured.

That father's kindness was what I found.

He is a gentle husband, father, and son.

I am his wife, mother, and yet child.

How they could be, yet divided into two

As long as you live, find a solution.'

ANTIOCHUS: Your time ceased Prince, better answer or expire.

PERICLES: Oh! King, some love to hear their own sins, as Kings are Earth's gods they do as they wish. All this is the love of females. And hence let me love my head.

ANTIOCHUS: (in a loud voice) Bravo!

You've found the meaning. Mercifully I'd talk fair to you Young man, you've forty

days to re-live. Until then you can entertain your head.

PERICLES: (*angrily*) How generous you are my Lord, here ruling a hypocrite, you and she (king'sdaughter)are serpents, breeding poison. She's pleasing you as a husband not as a father. Shame to your sin. Farewell! Antiochus.

(Exit)

ANTIOCHUS: (In a loud voice) Who will attend us there?

(Enters Thaliard.)

THALIARD: Your Highness!

ANTIOCHUS: Thaliard, you hold our secrecy, you shall be promoted for your faithfulness. You must kill the Prince of Tyre regarding my hatred.

THALIARD: It's done my Lord.

(Enters Messenger)

MESSENGER: My Lord, Prince of Tyre has fled.

(Exit.)

ANTIOCHUS: (To Thaliard) Never return unless you say "Prince Pericles is dead".

(Thaliard Exit.)

SCENE 2

(Tyre, A Room in the Palace; Enters Pericles with his Lords)

PERICLES: Let's no one disturb us. I used to be a familiar guest in Antioch but I don't honour King Antiochus anymore because of his misdeeds. We shall punish him before he does.

(Enters Helicanus with other Lords praising the Prince.)

PERICLES: Leave us! (Him and Helicanus)

PERICLES: I went to Antioch, against the face of death to wed a beauty. She was glorious, whose face is beyond wonders. But a sin found by me of the father and daughter. Is the princess worthy of the bloodshed? The darkness of lust has taken over them. Though I found this, war has blown.

HELICANUS: Alas! My Lord.

PERICLES: *(scared) My* sleep has gone and I am dreaming of blood. How I'll stop this war!

HELICANUS: My Lord, Antiochus is after you. Never knew, will it be a public war or private treason. My Lord, go travel for a while. Rest leave on Destiny. Amen I'll direct Tyre faithfully.

PERICLES: I don't doubt you but will he take advantage of my absence?

HELICANUS: We'll serve our blood for Tyre, My Lord.

PERICLES: I'll turn now for travel then. I'm looking for you and Tarsus for information. I'm grateful for my subjects. At this time, the loyalty of subjects will be shown.

(Exit.)

SCENE 3

(Tyre. An Antechamber in Palace; Enters Thaliard)

THALIARD: So this is Tyre and here I must slit Pericles' throat or else I'll lose mine. He must be a wise man to know the secret.

(Enter Helicanus, Escanes, with other Lords.)

HELICANUS: You shall not get what you need Sir, the Prince of Tyre has gone to travel.

THALIARD: What! The king has gone!

HELICANUS: I'll give some light when he departs. Being at Antioch, he was in grief, why, unknown to me.

THALIARD: I pray not to be hanged now or I would, anyway, I'll present myself.

HELICANUS: You shall leave for now, Sir.

(Exit.)

SCENE 4

(Tarsus. A Room in the Governor's House. Enter Cleon the Governor of Tarsus, with Dionyza his wife and others.)

CLEON: My Dionyza, Let's rest here.

(Enters a Lord)

LORD: Where's the lord governor?

CLEON: Your Highness!

LORD: We have described, upon our neighbourhood shore. A portly sail of ships are wrecked.

CLEON: Go tell their general we attend him here, to know for what he comes and from where and what he seeks for.

LORD: I go, My Lord!

(Exit.)

(Enter Pericles with Attendants.)

PERICLES: We are here for your love my Lord. We pray to the Lord.

CLEON: Welcome, Your Grace!

(The Same. A Hall of State. A Banquet prepared. Enter the King and Knights from tilting Thaisa, Ladies, Lords, and Attendants.)

KING: Dear daughter, My Princess, and all the honourable persons here. Please, enjoy this marvellous feast.

KNIGHTS: We are honoured.

THAISA: My father desires to know more about you.

PERICLES: I am Pericles, the Prince of Tyre. I am well educated in arts and arms. I look forward to new adventures in the world. Unfortunately our ship wracked and I am here. My gratitude to the King and You.

KING: You're the best among all, Prince. We all should depart for rest now.

PERICLES: Your Grace.

(Exit.)

SCENE 5

(Tyre, A Room in a Palace, enters Pericles.)

LORDS: (Praising the King)

PERICLES: I've been tested by fate but it gifted me my beloved princess, Marina. (To the Lords) The shadow of dark Clouds is disappearing. I'm looking forward to welcoming my loyalties to bless the princess and celebrate today's Feast.

LORDS: Your Highness!

(The feast begins with grandeur. The kingdom awaits to take a look at their beautiful princess. Enters Pericles with the queen and Marina. Lords praising the newborn.)

PERICLES: My golden angel with glittery eyes, who inspires my spirit of hope. I'm blessed by lord's goodness. May good God preserve you my child. She'll reign this glorious land. Amen.

(The next moment a sharp sword pierces the prince's body and it slit the baby's throat.)

NEW WIFE: Long live the King! May long reign the Queen!

(Exit)

XV

LOVE'S ILLUSION: A DREAMER'S DANCE - TAOCHIRENLA LONGKUMER

SCENE 1

(The scene is set in the Southwest countryside of England in a place called Devon, where luscious trees and greenery fill the surroundings. A place far from the hustle and bustle of city life, a home to people who choose to live a simple life. Antonio professes his love to Rosie who has been the centre of his gaze since the moment they met)

ANTONIO: (Talking to himself) Rosie, oh dearest Rosie, Cupid has shot an arrow right through my heart, and you have become the muse of my existence. Just the sight of you makes me weak in the knees, your smile lights up the room, and even your laugh is contagious. Although you may not feel the same about me, a piece of you will reside in my heart, forever and always.

(Enters Rosie)

ANTONIO: Fairest damsel, where are you going? Spare me some time and bless me with your presence, for I have waited long enough to behold such a beautiful sight.

ROSIE: Keep your dreamy thoughts to yourself, my whereabouts are none of your business, and I hope we never cross paths again. You have done nothing but bring trouble into my life, and my name is now tarnished by your words.

ANTONIO: I have done nothing but love you from the bottom of my heart, your mere presence brings me peace. So I tell you, fairest Rosie, th-

ROSIE: Enough is enough Antonio! If you don't move away from my sight, I will make sure that you never see me again!

(Antonio, with a concerned look, runs away in the opposite direction and sits down under a tree for a nap.)

ROSIE: (*In a loud, frustrated tone*) Time and time again, I have warned him not to pester me with his useless thoughts and dreams, but yet he still manages to get on my nerves by speaking nonsense, not only to me but to everyone in the village. I am through with him trying to sway me off my feet; he is nothing but a scoundrel who professes what he cannot practise.

(Isaac and Sophie enter.)

SOPHIE: Rosie, what are you doing out here? Weren't you on your way to the market?

ROSIE: Yes, I was, but that scoundrel Antonio distracted me. Anyways, where are the two of you heading off to?

ISAAC: We're on our way to meet your father; it's been a while since we last visited.

ROSIE: Oh, alright then. I'll see you when I'm back.

(Isaac and Sophie exits)

ROSIE: (Talking to herself) God forbid I speak this way, but my heart sways to the tune of Isaac's voice, my sister's husband. My heart flutters when I see him, and I know it's impossible, but I wish it were me instead who married him and called him mine. But such thoughts are just foolishness as he is nothing but an in-law to me, the father of my sister's coming child and a lover to my only sister. So how could I ever betray her by having such thoughts?I must get to the market fast, else the good stock will be over.

(Exeunt)

SCENE 2

ANTONIO: (To himself)I have been faithful to Rosie, loving her wholeheartedly with the hope that one day she might notice me, even from afar and reciprocate my feelings. For two years, I have waited patiently for her to return the love I have always held for her, but it seems all for naught as she now despises me even more than before. It is time I take matters into my own hands and make her mine.

(Antonio exits on his way to meet a witch.)

WITCH: What brings a young man as handsome as you to my abode? Do you seek to fulfil a desire with a touch of magic?

ANTONIO: I am here to request a love potion. I am in love with someone who does not love me in return, and I have decided to act upon it. Kind witch, could you grant me a love-for-love potion?

WITCH: Every action has its consequence, be mindful of what you are about to do, for there is no antidote to this potion.

ANTONIO: My mind is made up, and my heart knows its desire so you need not worry.

WITCH: As you wish, but don't come back running if anything goes awry.

(The witch enchants the potion and hands Antonio the vial.)

ANTONIO: (Hands her a bag of silver coins)Thank you.

(Outside Rosie's house, Antonio speaks to one of her servants)

ANTONIO: You know where to put this right? Do as I instruct, ensure she drinks it and I shall reward you handsomely.

SERVANT: Yes sir, I will see to it that Madame Rosie alone sips from her cup with the potion. (The servant discreetly pours the contents of the vial into Rosie's cup while she is engaged in a conversation with Sophie)

SERVANT: As you have commanded, I have done. Now we wait for Madame Rosie to seek you out.

(Antonio thanks the servant and hands him twenty silver coins.)

(Inside the house, Isaac notices a glass of juice on the table and drinks a sip, unaware it has been laced with the potion.)

ISAAC: This juice has an odd taste...(He starts feeling dizzy and collapses to the floor.)

(When Isaac awakens, his emotions are in turmoil, and he finds himself irresistibly drawn to Antonio, pursuing him in the hope of mutual affection.)

(Exeunt)

SCENE 3

ANTONIO: (To himself) Rosie must be here by now. I hope she will finally see me for the man I am. I have waited for this moment for so long, and though I've had a hand at altering my fate, I'm glad it will finally come to pass.

(Sees Isaac running happily towards him)

ISAAC: Antonio! I've been searching for you far and wide. I have something to confess. It may surprise you, and I might even sound foolish, but ever since I awoke, I've been overwhelmed with affection for you. You have taken my breath away. Standing here beside you, I realise that you are my sea, my sunshine, the star and the moon. Nothing compares to you, and you alone can fill the void in my heart. I hope you accept me as I am and love me just as much as I love you.

ANTONIO: Nonsense! Are you bewitched? Why do you talk such madness, dear brother? (Realises Isaac might have drunk from the cup meant for Rosie) Oh no, treachery! What has become of my fate? I would rather remain alone than accept you as my lover. Get out of my sight!

ISAAC: Why won't you accept my love? I will treat you well and love you sincerely. Can't you see I'm completely yours? (Steps closer to embrace Antonio)

(Antonio dodges the embrace and flees)

ANTONIO: What am I to do now? This isn't how I wanted things to end. I tried to change my fate, and now I've ruined everything. Perhaps I shouldn't have meddled with destiny and none of this chaos would have ensued. I thought I could- (Isaac embraces him from behind; Antonio screams and suddenly wakes up, sweaty, shaking and breathless) It was all a crazy dream! Perhaps it was a sign not to tamper with my destiny. I must leave; it's grown quite dark. Thank heavens it was just a silly dream.

(Exeunt)

XVI
A PAINFUL DILEMMA - THARSORIN HONGCHUI

SCENE 1

(Vienna, on a busy street, shouting of vendors, children crying, chariots galloping.)

(Enter Duke and George)

DUKE: Has my message being conveyed to Lord Angelo

GEORGE: Yes, my lord. All the arrangement has been made, not a word of your plans will be known, even lord Angelo himself. But...my lord; do you really have to guide yourself as a friar!

DUKE: Nobody will suspect me this way, besides it's the right time to test Angelo's loyalty to the court, furthermore his connection and scheming can no longer be set aside.

GEORGE: May favour be upon you my lord, I shall depart from here.

DUKE: Indeed. Make haste, let not your absence be noticed by my loyal subjects.

(George leaves while the Duke continues for his destination to the monastery. Peter knocked the door of the monastery breathlessly from the run.)

PETER: Sister Isabella, I have brought urgent news for you. Please do hear me out, it's from your dearest brother James. (Door opens from Inside)

ISABELLA: Peter, what news do you bring? Your face looks mischievous and full of secrets. Don't tell me it's another one of you and my brother silly games.

PETER: Isabella, my friend, get ready for a story that will shock and amuse you. It's about your brother, James, who got caught in a really tough situation.

ISABELLA: Please, Peter, tell me what happened to James. Don't keep me in suspense, I'm scared.

PETER: Don't worry Isabella, I'll tell you the story with a mix of dark comedy. James got Juliet pregnant and unfortunately, it is against the law to do so. He is in the mud right now!

ISABELLA: Oh no! What will happen to James now? I'm so scared for him.

PETER: I'm sorry Isabella, but the punishment for James' mistake is death. It's a harsh world we live in.

ISABELLA: Death? Peter, we have to find a way to save him. We have to beg for his life. Maybe there's some mercy in the hearts of those in power.

PETER: Isabella, you're as noble as a star. Do you have a plan? Even though I'm usually full of wit and charm, I for once cannot help you with this. If you do have, please, share your thoughts.

ISABELLA: Peter, what's my brothers take on this? What if we cannot do anything about it; because other than going to Sir Angelo and pleading with him to show some mercy in person, l have no idea what l can do for my beloved brother. So, I will go to Angelo, the person in charge here, and plead for mercy. Pray that it will be successful.

PETER: Great plan, Isabella! But be careful, Angelo is strict and follows the rules. You have to be careful and not make any mistakes that could harm your brother.

ISABELLA: Don't worry Peter, I'll approach Angelo respectfully and carefully. I'll appeal to his sense of fairness and understanding. Maybe I can convince him to show mercy.

PETER: You're a ray of hope Isabella, shining in the darkness. I'll be by your side, supporting you and using my wit to help you.

(Isabellamurmuring prayers)

Almighty God above, I come before you with a heavy heart, not only to plead for mercy for my dear brother James but also to ask for forgiveness for the actions he has committed. I acknowledge the wrongdoing and the pain it has caused. I pray for thy strength to convey my sincerest apologies to Angelo and to seek understanding and forgiveness for James' transgressions. May my words reflect the remorse in my heart and may they touch Angelo's soul, opening a path towards redemption and healing for all involved. Amen.

(Concludes her prayer and leavest for the castle of Sir Angelo)

SCENE 2

(A sick old lady asking medicine from the medicine seller being shunned away was noticed by the Duke)

DUKE: Good day, good madam. I couldn't help but notice that you seem troubled. Is there anything I can do to assist you?

OLD LADY: Oh, kind friar, I've been shunned away by the medicine seller. He refuses to help me with my ailments.

FRIAR: Fear not, for I shall lend you a helping hand. I have some alms with me which may be of use to you. Furthermore, good madam, it is my duty and passion to help those in need. (Gives some alms to the old lady)

OLD LADY: I couldn't thank you more, Oh! Kind Friar, I shall go on my way without delay.

FRIAR: Please do so, good madam.

(Old lady exit)

ISABELLA: Pardon me for interrupting, but I couldn't help but witness this act of kindness. You truly embody compassion, dear friar.

FRIAR: Thank you, kind lady. It is my duty to assist those in need. May we all strive to show empathy and support to one another.

ISABELLA: True indeed. But it is so rare to see people giving out or lending a hand to those in need without expecting anything in return.

(Isabella laments melancholically)

FRIAR: Something seems to be troubling you, fair lady. If I may ask what troubles are you going through?

(Contemplates, but choose to say it as they share the same religious beliefs and compassion)

ISABELLA: You might find it absurd, even funny to an extent but, I'm going to meet sir Angelo to plead leniency for my brother's misdeeds.

FRIAR: It must be a serious issue if you're going to meet Sir Angelo.

ISABELLA: True indeed. My good brother's only mistake was making his fiancée pregnant before their marriage; now, with the ruling of Vienna by Sir Angelo, the punishment for my brother's sin can no longer be resolved.

(The Duke ruminates deeply)

FRIAR: Why so fair lady?

ISABELLA: Sir Angelo is determined to set things straight and act for a proper cause as Vienna has been too corrupted over the past years. He has started ruling out the adulterous folks as early as yesterday and has started his judgement.

FRIAR: Such sad news! Good grief

(Isabella hums)

FRIAR: Fair lady I shall not delay you further of your appointment. You may go ahead for your purpose, but worry not as I have established some friendship inside the court through frequent visits and have some encounters with the Duke himself. I shall see what I can do to help you.

ISABELLA: Thank you so much kind friar, you have been the kindest soul that I ever met.

FRIAR: You praise me too much, kind lady! I promise to keep you informed of any news and share the location of our next meeting. Until then, take care and may our paths cross again soon.

(Isabella and the Duke both leave for their own destination.)

SCENE 3

(Inside the court of the Duke, Angelo sits in the middle with his subjects surrounding him. One of the ministers reports the list of adulterous and unscrupulous people that have been captured and their crimes.)

ANGELO: Good work my loyal subjects. Meeting is dismissed. George!!!

GEORGE: Here at your service Sir Angelo.

ANGELO: Have you got any news where our beloved Duke is? Also his reason for leaving the great Vienna under my command?

GEORGE: Sir Angelo! His grace has departed for England with the belief of your mighty leadership and judgmental skills. He has trust in you.

ANGELO: Is that so? I am pleased to hear that his grace trusts me, but why depart?

GEORGE: His grace told me that he wanted to take a break from the court matters to live a quiet and peaceful life for the time being .He had wanted to travel around and see the beauties of the world with nothing to hold him back.

ANGELO: Might be true for his majesty .He might have been tied down with the duties of the court and of course the unruly folks of Vienna. They are getting out of hand, this is the right time to straighten out everything! His grace has far been too lenient and good for the likes of the unscrupulous citizens. I might as well do his work.

(George listens silent)

ANGELO: You may go for your duties George. You don't have to stand here all day like you did with the Duke; Also while on your way please do call Sir Edmund, I have some matters to discuss with him.

GEORGE: Then I shall proceed to my duties sir Angelo.

(George went out. He greeted and informed Sir Edmund who was discussing some matters, regarding Sir Angelo's recent punishment to James. Door opens and Sir Edmund enter)

ANGELO: Ah! Edmund, my loyal friend, great timing! What do you think of my recent act? Was it what the Duke should have done from before or do you find me doing this as an offence?

SIR EDMUND: Good Sir! Your recent act has certainly caused quite the commotion. Some might say you've taken a leap of faith, while others might think you've gone off the deep end. But sir, who am I to judge?

ANGELO: What a sharp tongue you have got, but I like your answer. From now onwards my dear friend, you are my advisor and loyal subject.

SIR EDMUND: I couldn't thank you more sir.

ANGELO: You don't have to thank me, all you need to do is stay faithful and cover up my loopholes whenever needed.

(Angelo dismissed Sir Edmund while smiling to himself. A voice informs Angelo of a lady arrival

Door opens again and Isabella comes in)

ISABELLA: Sir Angelo, This is your humble subject Isabella requesting your compassion for my brother James. He deeply regrets his actions and seeks forgiveness. With your kindness and benevolence please reduce his sentence.

ANGELO: Fair lady, I understand your plea. However, I am unable to make a decision at this moment. Please return tomorrow, and we can continue this discussion with proper consideration.

ISABELLA: Thank you sir, I understand that you need time to consider my request but please do consider my humble prayer. Your humble subject shall come back tomorrow as you suggested.

(Isabella leaves with a heavy heart, feeling dejected. Angelo mused to himself how great it feels to be in power while the Duke reached out to Marianna in the small town where she was exiled secretly without anyone knowing, promising her a deal of marrying her to Angelo if she agrees to help him . Night descent.)

Sir Angelo, I have come back again as agreed upon yesterday. Please, I beg of you, show leniency towards my brother James. He has made a grave mistake, but I implore you to spare his life.

ANGELO: Isabella, the law is clear. Adultery is a serious offence, and it must be punished accordingly. I cannot simply turn a blind eye to such transgressions.

ISABELLA: But Sir Angelo, there must be some way to save him from this cruel fate. I beseech you to consider mercy and forgiveness.

ANGELO: Isabella, I understand your plea, but the law must be upheld. However, if you truly wish to save your brother, there is a way. If you yield yourself to me, I will spare James' life.

ISABELLA: Sir Angelo, I am a chaste nun, devoted to my faith. I cannot compromise my virtue for the sake of another. I cannot accept your proposition.

(Marianna, who had come all the way from her exile through the help of the Duke, overheard the conversation and rushed in)

MARIANNA: Angelo, how can you be so heartless? Isabella is right to refuse your indecent proposal. You claim to uphold the law, but your actions are unjust.

ANGELO: Marianna, this does not concern you. I have no intention of marrying you now that you have lost your dowry. You are to be in exile right now, and there is no changing that.

MARIANNA: Angelo, listen to me. Miraculously, my dowry has been recovered from the shipwreck. We can still be married, and I can prove my worthiness to you.

ANGELO: You were not worthy of me before and even more now that I'm at this stage

MARIANNA: You hurt my feelings Angelo though you knew I'm mad for your love and can do anything to achieve that.

(Isabella excuse herself while Marianna and Angelo were in heated conversation)

ANGELO: Please leave Marianna while I'm being nice, we shall have no further discussion regarding this ridiculous marriage.

MARIANNA: Have you forgotten how good my father was to you before he died in the shipwreck. He treated you like a son. Angelo! Please do remember how you promised him to take good care of me .Is this how you repay him after all the things he had done for you.

ANGELO: Enough Marianna please leave before I lose my patience and call the guards. And for once behave like a lady should.

(Marianna leaves visibly upset, crying while Angelo rubs his head and frowns tiredly. Marianna noticed Isabella's silhouette as she was on her way out and approached her with tears in her eyes.)

MARIANNA: Isabella, I'm sorry for what just happened. Angelo's words hurt me deeply. I don't know what to do.

ISABELLA: Oh, Marianna, it's not your fault. . Let's find a way to support each other and navigate through this difficult situation together.

MARIANNA: You won't accept Angelo's request right?

ISABELLA: Never sister. It is against my principles to do so.

MARIANNA: Truth to be told, a kind young friar helped me free of my exile. He has some connections with the Duke and has helped me with my dowries also. Do you think a friar can convince a Duke who is travelling to help me or do you think he is the Duke himself?

ISABELLA: Well, Sister Marianna, it's hard to say for sure. But a kind young friar with connections to the Duke could definitely be influential.

MARIANNA: True indeed. Don't worry too much sister, help will come eventually for the kind soul. Let's part our way from here. We shall meet someday if luck favours us. It was good talking to you.

(Isabella and Marianna departs)

SCENE 4

(Angelo talking to himself in his chamber consumed with greed for power.)

ANGELO: Ah, the taste of power is like a sweet nectar, intoxicating and irresistible. As I establish my influence within the court, my ambitions grow stronger, burning like a fire within me. The throne, the ultimate symbol of authority, calls out to me, whispering promises of limitless control and dominance. I plot and scheme, weaving a web of deceit and manipulation, with each thread carefully calculated to secure my path to the throne. Every move is calculated, every word spoken with purpose. But my ambitions do not stop there. I yearn for more than just power. To solidify my nobility, I devise a plan to marry the Duke's sister. Such a union would elevate my status, making me untouchable, invincible. With her by my side, I would possess not only the throne but also the loyalty and respect of the noble families. I shall seize every opportunity that presents itself. The world will soon witness my rise, as I ascend to the apex of authority, ruling with an iron fist.

(Inside a small house, a town where Marianna was exiled. Duke with George while the latter knocks the door. Door opens up with Marianna gaping in surprise.)

MARIANNA: Greetings your grace

(Doing a curtsy)

DUKE: No need for formalities, good lady! You may rise.

MARIANNA: Welcome to my humble home, your grace, what brings your grand presence here to this small town. Is there anything that I can do for you?

DUKE: Good lady, I have heard of your family misfortune! My condolences to you.

MARIANNA: Thank you, your grace.

DUKE: I see that you recognise me though I'm in guise .That is so sharp of you.

MARIANNA: Thank you, your grace, for your praise, but who doesn't know your name and face in this great Vienna, your compassion and kindness is known to all.

DUKE: Let me go to the point good lady; I have a proposition for you: Your task is to come back with me, I have a chariot outside waiting for you, You have to help me fulfil some task relating to Angelo whom I heard you are fond of, your fiancé, I suppose...And in turn I will reinstate your dowry, free you from your exile and even your marriage with Angelo will be secured. What do you think?

MARIANNA: I cannot thank you more for your benevolence, your grace. But, what task Am I supposed to take up, if I may ask.

DUKE: George will inform you of your task when the time comes, the carriage will take you to an inn where you shall stay and wait for your task.

MARIANNA: I shall do as you say, your grace.

DUKE: Farewell good Lady

(Inside a luxurious room, a big mirror stood facing Lady Christina. Two maids combing and styling her long tress while she relaxes, a knock ensued on the door, a maid came in with a click.)

MAID: My lady, Sir Angelo has come to seek your audience .He is currently in the garden waiting for your arrival.

LADY CHRISTINA: okay enough with the styling; I'll go and hear what he has in store for me.

(Stands up with a swish sound and proceed for the garden)

ANGELO: Good day to you my lady! Your beauty never fades, still blooming ever so fresh like wildflowers, free and spirited. My Lady, as we stroll through this magnificent garden, I am in awe of your beauty. You are like a rare blossom, standing out amidst the vibrant colours around us.

LADY CHRISTINA: Oh, Angelo, your words flatter me. This garden pales in comparison to your sweet compliments.

ANGELO: It is not just your beauty that captivates me, but also your spirit. I truly admire your beauty, graceful nature, kind heart, sweet demeanour, and not to forget your lovely smile. I am truly starstruck by you. I cannot forget you, though I tried to .Your sweet smile continues to linger on my mind in the death of night. She ,here I Am prompted by love to ask for your hand though in absence of his grace, your only kin .My sorrowful heart will be finally relieved if only you accept my love and think of the future ahead with me by your side. I no longer will have lonely nights for your sweet perfume and presence shall fill the air, soothing my aching soul. You have entrapped me since the first day I saw you at the coronation of your brother. Since then u have become my dream. Though our encounters were short most of the time I still remember all the encounters. If you and I are together, we will create a life filled with love, happiness, and prosperity. I promise to cherish and protect you always. So, if you could do me the favour of becoming your one and only, my wish will be fulfilled and I will be over the moon. What do you say my lady?

LADY CHRISTINA: Sir Angelo, thank you for appreciation, your words touched my heart. I am filled with joy at the thought of you thinking so highly of me, I really do appreciate your gesture; however, I would like to wait for my brother's approval before proceeding with any step as he is the only close kin left of me. Until then I cannot give you my answer as you desire. Please do not be offended by my words Sir Angelo.

ANGELO: My dear Lady Christina, Your words don't offend me at all, though I'm deeply saddened with your response. I understand your concern as his grace indeed is your closest kin. I am in the wrong, rushing for your response, it's just that my mind and soul wants to stay with you always and cannot dare to think of my future without you, it just seems so bleak. So, I dare to express my feelings in a rush. Sorry for my rudeness and absurdity in expressing my feelings. But, if you do ever change your mind you can always come for me and I will welcome you with open arms. For now I will take my leave, enjoy your evening.

(Both Christina and Angelo depart. Inside the monastery, George and The Duke sits in a table with two chairs, a pile of books relating to historical accounts and religious texts were scattered)

DUKE: What news have you brought this time George?

GEORGE: Your Grace Sir Angelo has made his move, he has appointed Sir Edmund as his advisor and next in line to him.

DUKE: Just as I expected of him, did a fair lady come to seek his audience.

GEORGE: Yes, a lady, probably a chaste nun, came to plead mercy for her brother James who is set to a death sentence for impregnating his fiancé before marriage after 5 days.

DUKE: Any news from our Insider?

GEORGE: Yes, our Insider also informed that Marianna came just in time to see Angelo coercing Lady Isabella to lie with him but was rejected as it was against her principle, though it was the only way to save her beloved brother from his punishment.

Marianna, as you have arranged, went to Angelo claiming to have miraculously regained her dowries from the shipwreck. She is all set out to marry Angelo and has also befriended Lady Isabella outside the castle, where they talk for some time.

DUKE: That's good news. I have waited so long to uncover Angelo's fake respect for me and his loyalty. It's high time to set things in order. Let him do his moves without rushing, at the right time I will cut his powers and make him experience what it felt like to be plotting against me.

GEORGE: Your Grace, Angelo was also seen flattering and sending gifts to your sister Lady Christina. Though not openly, Angelo has also expressed his desire to marry her ladyship.

(Wooing my sister, trying to bed Lady Isabella, exiling Lady Marianna, trying to curb my power and position. So much time and strength he has mused the Duke.)

DUKE: Keep monitoring his moves George, and make sure to keep Lady Marianna near the castle where Isabella can easily spot her on the fourth night, out of desperation Lady Isabella will surely come again for Angelo. All the three of us should meet there and then and there I shall decide my next move.

(Maybe Lady Marianna might be aware of some of his moves, since her first encounter with lady Isabella was set by him.)

Let's depart for now.

(Both the Duke and George stood up and George left the monastery.)

SCENE 5

(A knock on the door with Peter's voice shouting for Isabella.

Door opens with a click and Isabella with swollen eyes greets Lucio)

ISABELLA: What shall we do Peter, I've been praying every day for divine intervention but nothing seems to be working out. Angelo is strong minded and won't heed my plea unless I lie with him, what can be done now. We're hopeless.

PETER: Death might not suit such a lovely personality like your brother. He is too young to be on his deathbed, moreover he is set to be a 'papa' to his unborn child. Such a sad ending he has got, were he to die.

ISABELLA: I know Peter, he is reaping what he sowed .Had he not done this we would not have faced this issue. Though I love him I cannot ignore his misdeeds.

PETER: True sister Isabella, but your brother's life cannot be ignored. James has asked me to tell you to acquiesce to Sir Angelo's request, he cannot bear the thought of leaving his child and Juliet to face the society's criticism alone. He said he will make up with whatever you needed even to the point of supporting you until your last breath were you to help him this time .

ISABELLA: I will see what I can do. But, I cannot betray my conscience .I will plead mercy to Sir Angelo again .You shall not be too optimistic about it.

PETER: I know sister Isabella, farewell.

(Outside the castle, Marianna and the friar could be seen talking with carriages behind them. The guards standing on both sides of the gate)

ISABELLA: Good to see both of you together. Lady Marianna, kind Friar, what brings you both here?

MARIANNA: I'm here to seek an audience with Sir Angelo, my supposed fiancé, but I'm being shunned out. This is the friar that helped me with my exile, he is a relative of the Duke that I was talking about the last time we met. If I'm not wrong to say, both of you might have met before according to your reaction and greetings.

FRIAR: True indeed, we have met before Lady Marianna. Maybe lady luck must be favouring us or maybe all of us were just destined to meet from the beginning itself.

ISABELLA: Maybe finally fortune may be favouring the misfortune .But what are you doing here, kind Friar?

FRIAR: I Am going to visit the prison to pray and counsel for those in need of redemption or have a change of heart. I can help you check out how your brother is, how he is doing inside the cell if you want me to! And we can think of a solution after that. What do you think, good lady?

ISABELLA: Please do so kind Friar, my gratefulness will know no bounds. I am deeply touched by your help.

(Tears rolling down her cheeks)

MARIANNA: Such a great burden you have got. My sympathy goes for you dear sister". Our lives are really messed up. The man I loved wants to lie with you while my feelings were left unnoticed, such a cruel man he is, disregarding me as soon as my value is over. Such a life we have got.

(Marianna lamented and spoke out loud. Suddenly she shook her head, her eyes twinkling.)

How about you go inside first, tell Angelo that you have agreed to his request, and I will switch places with you. I will lie with him pretending to be you, it might not be so good to deceive him but, what more options are we left if not these. It will look better as I Am still his flangeway. Do you suggest it my dear sister?

ISABELLA: Really! My dear sister.

MARIANNA: Yes, no worries, besides he was my fiancé before and I love him .So rest assured.

ISABELLA: Thank you so much dear Marianna. I will be immensely and truly grateful to you if you are willing to do this for me even though you might be implicated in this mess.

(Isabella continue showing her gratitude while she nods her head to the Friar)

FRIAR: Since this problem is solved we better proceed with it. I will go inside and inform your brother not to worry, Lady Isabella you shall go inside and do so as Lady Marianna has suggested. Let's try to do everything to the best of our ability since we are in this together .We all shall meet up tomorrow morning for further decisions.

(The two ladies hums together, Isabella went inside first while the Duke and Marianna remained standing)

MARIANNA: Your Grace, please keep your promises to me and I will do my part faithfully.

FRIAR: You need not worry Lady, I always keep my word, now let's go on and fulfil our duties.

(Both of them dispersed. Inside the castle, Angelo sits in a luxurious chair while Isabella speaks to him. Two of his attendants tending his tea and snacks)

ISABELLA: Sir Angelo, your humble subject has done what was asked of me, can you now please release my brother James from the prison, he also has known his mistake, it shall never be repeated, they will also get married by the end of this month, therefore I beg of you to please spare my brother's life.

DUKE: Lady Isabella, I understand your plight but now the Whole Vienna has known of your brother's misdeeds, though I wish to spare his life, the issued degree can no longer be retracted, so even if I wish to help you, my ministers will not agree to it.

LADY ISABELLA: But Sir Angelo, What about your promise, was it just an empty word to coerce me. Please I beg of you, I will never ever forget your favour for the rest of my life. Please help me!

ANGELO: There are no more other ways? I can no longer help you. Your brother will be executed this evening as planned. There will be no more discussion on this topic, you can leave, thank you for your service.

(Isabella sobbed and exited the door while Friar and Lady Marianna stood outside the castle.)

MARIANNA: Is everything settled? Has Angelo decided to spare your dearest brother Claudio of his sentence?

ISABELLA: Sir Angelo has gone back on his promise. My brother's life can no longer be saved. But still my gratitude and appreciation went to you two. Thank you so much for your help.

(Isabella's sobbing continues)

FRIAR: Save your tears Lady Isabella, I'm going to make sure your brother's life will be saved, just wait until the evening on the execution ground, the Duke is sure bound to return at that time, He will bring justice for you. So, fret not, Lady Isabella.

ISABELLA: But, even if the Duke returns, will he understand my plight, even worse my brother's? He will still choose to believe his ministers and Angelo, after all they are his subjects.

FRIAR: Worry not, I can assure you that your brother will be saved. I have personally met the Duke himself, you will also come to know how amiable and compassionate he is. Moreover, Lady Marianna will help you at that point. So, go home in peace.

(All three of them dispersed on the execution ground, Angelo sits on the podium while Claudio's head lays in the guillotine, guards and crowd gathers to watch the execution.)

ANGELO: Sir Edmund, you can address the crowd and tell them what he did wrong and tell them how I planned to set things straight for the people of Vienna with him as an example, tell them how' I, Angelo, will take up the role of punishing the unruly folks in place of the Duke.

(Sir Edmund addresses the crowd)

SIR EDMUND: Elder, friends, children and all the people of great Vienna! Today, I stand before you in place of our esteemed sir Angelo. Everybody has gone wild therefore, the Sir has taken the example of this man lying here whose good name is Claudio, his sin was impregnating his fiancé before marriage, as a result his crime can only be addon with death. This will ensure that justice prevails and order is restored. Together, we will create a better future for the people of Vienna.

(Concludes his speech and steps back. Cheers, music, trumpets ensued indicating the return of the Duke.)

DUKE: What grand occasion is going on here for my citizens to have come and gathered here, and why is there a man in the guillotine? Is something going on without my knowledge dear Angelo?

(Turn back and look at the crowd, Isabella gasps in surprise while the Duke shows an amused smile.)

ANGELO: Greetings Your Grace, Welcome back, I wasn't informed of your homecoming, were to know, your humble ministers and I would have prepared a feast for you.

DUKE: No need for the trouble Angelo, But what is going on here?

ANGELO: Your Grace, Angelo has committed the crime of impregnating his fiancé before marriage as a result he is being punished, to serve as an example for others not to follow in his footsteps. It is not worth your time so why don't I do the honour of escorting you back to the castle.

DUKE: Nothing to worry about me, I'm perfectly healthy. But I have a question for you Sir Angelo!

ANGELO: Ask away, your grace.

DUKE: A report has reached me that you have exiled and dissolved your marriage agreement with Lady Marianna, and refuse to wed her, you have also appointed Sir Edmund and several other ministers to be your Ally without my knowledge. Is this what a loyal subject does?

(A lady rushed forward)

MARIANNA: Your Grace, I'm Lady Marianna, Sir Angelo's supposed fiancé. He has refused to acknowledge our marriage agreement though he and I have become one during a rendezvous night.

ANGELO: What gibberish are you talking about Lady Marianna? When did I lie with you, don't try to sow discord between his grace and me, you better go back and don't hinder my relationship with his grace.

DUKE: Lady Marianna, Do you have anything as evidence to prove your claim?

MARIANNA: Yes, your grace, this is the robe of Sir Angelo that I took, the night he slept with me.

ANGELO: What are you talking about! 1 never am in an enclosed space with you ,not to think a night with you, this is utterly impossible. And even if I did lie with someone, it won't be you.

MARIANNA: I had lady Isabella switch places with me and she can testify to it for me.

(Isabella and Juliet rushed forward and do a curtsey)

ISABELLA: Your grace, it is true that Marianna slept with Sir Angelo as his only solution for saving my brother was to lie with him and so the switching took place, but later he went back on his word and has decided to take my brother's life. But please, Your Grace, with utmost respect I beg of you to spare my brother from his punishment.

JULIET: Your Grace, please spare my fiancé life, we have done wrong and we would surely repent it , please don't deprived me and my unborn child the presence of a husband and father, we will serve you with loyalty and faithfulness for the rest of our lives were you to pardon our sins.

(Both Isabella and Juliet sobbed while the Duke ruminates)

DUKE: I have come up with a decision for all these problems and will announce it to you with all the crowd present here.

As Lady Marianna and Angelo were supposed to marry from the beginning, they will continue with the marriage.

(The Duke continues)

I wish to spare you Angelo, but I have several reports of you bribing the ministers and using unfair means to accumulate power and wealth, while you at the same time preach against those and punish them in public. Admitting your love for my sister while disregarding your fiancé, simultaneously, coercing Lady Isabella to lie with you. With such an act you are not fit to be a minister governing thousands of people. Henceforth I the Duke of Vienna dismissed you from your duties, now onwards you are just Angelo, a common man while lady Isabella former dowries will be restored along with a mansion for being of great help to me during the past months

(Marianna bows with gratitude, the crowd claps)

As for James he shall be freed of his sentence, but serve as a soldier for two years as a sign of repentance. While Lady Isabella, a true lady of virtue with the heart of gold, full of faith, love and respect has gained my admiration, and if your heart agrees, I would like to wed you in a holy matrimony

(Crowd dispersed)

XVII
LOST IN LINKS - ABHINAV V

SCENE 1

(The stage is a sleek, modern control centre within a high-tech security firm. Digital screens line the walls, casting a soft blue glow across the room. Othello, a formidable figure with a strong presence, stands beside Desdemona, a confident and compassionate woman who commands respect. Their camaraderie is evident as they engage in a lively discussion about the latest cyber threats. In the shadows, Roderigo, his yearning for Desdemona unfulfilled, observes with a mixture of envy and longing.)

NARRATOR: (Setting the scene) Step into the heart of the digital fortress, a space where lines of code and algorithms rule. The room hums with the energy of technology, and the soft blue glow from the screens bathes the characters in its digital aura. Meet Othello, our guardian of cyber security, a modern-day knight in digital armour. His presence alone exudes strength and confidence. Beside him is Desdemona, a diplomat of justice, navigating the virtual battlegrounds with grace and determination. Her eyes reflect the screens' glow as she points at data streams filled with digital threats.

DESDEMONA: (energetically pointing at a computer screen) Othello, this breach is a potential catastrophe waiting to happen. Our clients are at risk, and we can't afford to let them down.

OTHELLO: (assuredly, his eyes on the screens) Desdemona, don't worry. We'll track down the digital culprits and fortify our defences. Together, we're an unbreakable firewall, protecting not just our clients but the digital realm itself.

(Rodrigo, concealed in the dimly lit corner, clutches his fists in jealousy. His feelings of longing and frustration intensify as he watches Desdemona and Othello work seamlessly together.)

RODERIGO: (in a hushed tone, frustration in his voice) Desdemona, why does he get all the attention? Why can't you see me for who I am? I've been here, supporting you from the shadows, and yet you only have eyes for him.

NARRATOR: (observing Roderigo) In the hidden recesses of the control centre, Roderigo's envy simmers like a digital virus, infecting his every thought. He yearns for Desdemona's affection, believing that he could be her shield in this digital battleground.

DESDEMONA: (turning to Othello with determination) Othello, we can't underestimate the enemy. Our clients rely on us to keep their data secure and their trust intact. We have to be one step ahead of these cyber threats.

OTHELLO: (nodding, a sense of responsibility in his voice) You're right, Desdemona. The digital world is a battlefield, and we're the frontline defenders. Let's dig deep into the code, trace the threat's origin, and neutralise it.

(As Othello and Desdemona engage in their discussion, the audience witnesses not only their dedication to their work but also the unspoken bond between them. It's a partnership built on trust and shared purpose, but unbeknownst to them, it's a partnership that fuels Roderigo's inner turmoil.)

RODERIGO: (sighing, his voice filled with longing) If only you knew, Desdemona. If only you could see how much I care.

DESDEMONA: (Suddenly, with a warm smile) Roderigo, you've been such a great help. Your support means the world to me.

RODERIGO: (surprised, his heart racing.) Do you mean it?

DESDEMONA: (Genuinely) Of course, Roderigo. We're a team, and your dedication doesn't go unnoticed.

NARRATOR: (reflecting on the characters) In the heart of this digital fortress, emotions run as deep as the complex algorithms that power it. The stage is set for a drama that will explore the boundaries of trust, the dangers of jealousy, and the fragility of human hearts in the digital era.

(Addressing the audience) As the digital web begins to weave its intricate threads of suspicion and desire, remember that human hearts can be as vulnerable as any firewall in the age of technology. Stay tuned for the digital drama that's about to unfold.

SCENE 2

(The stage transitions to a sleek, modern office within the security firm. Othello and Desdemona continue to work diligently, engrossed in their tasks. Rodrigo, fuelled by jealousy and resentment, becomes a pawn in Iago's plan to exploit Roderigo's unrequited love for Desdemona.)

NARRATOR: (Setting the scene) the office is an extension of the digital battlefield, a place where cyber warriors strategize and execute their plans. Othello and Desdemona, immersed in their work, remain dedicated to their mission. The soft hum of technology is their constant companion.

OTHELLO: (focused, typing rapidly) Desdemona, we need to patch the vulnerabilities we discovered in the last breach. We must maintain the integrity of our clients' data.

DESDEMONA: (equally absorbed) Agreed, Othello. I'm running diagnostics to identify any potential weaknesses in our systems. We can't afford any slip-ups.

(Roderigo, lurking in the shadows, watches their dedication with growing frustration.)

RODERIGO: (muttering to himself, bitterness in his voice) They are always together, always working. She doesn't even notice me.

(Rodrigo's thoughts turn to Iago, a charming but enigmatic colleague known for his cunning ways. He approaches Iago, who wears a disarming smile.)

IAGO:(*smirking*) Roderigo, my friend, you seem troubled. What's eating at you?

Roderigo: (confident in Iago) It's Desdemona. She's always with Othello, and I can't stand it. I've been by her side for so long, and she doesn't even acknowledge me.

IAGO: (feigning concern) That's a tough spot to be in, Roderigo. But you see, there are ways to make her notice you.

RODERIGO: (Eagerly) What do you mean?

IAGO: (leaning in, a glint in his eye) My friend, in this digital age, information is power. Let's create a little illusion—a whisper in the digital winds that might just turn her attention your way.

(Iago's words plant the seeds of manipulation in Roderigo's mind. They begin their scheme, crafting fake rumours about Desdemona and Cassio.)

NARRATOR: (observing the plot) In the realm of deception, Iago's cunning intertwines with Roderigo's jealousy. Together, they fashion lies that seem real, blurring the line between truth and illusion.

RODERIGO: (*anxiously*) Iago, are you sure this will work? What if we're caught?

IAGO: (*confidently*) Trust me, Roderigo. In the digital world, perception is everything. We'll create an illusion so convincing that even Othello won't know what hit him.

(As Roderigo and Iago conspire, the tension in the office grows. Othello and Desdemona, unaware of the deception unfolding around them, remain committed to their mission.)

DESDEMONA: (to Othello) I think we've patched the vulnerabilities. Our client's data should be secure now.

OTHELLO: (Grateful) Thanks, Desdemona. Your dedication is invaluable.

NARRATOR: (describing Cassio) Meanwhile, in the backdrop of this digital drama stands Michael Cassio, a charismatic and trusted colleague of Othello and Desdemona. Known for his impeccable record and friendly demeanour, Cassio is highly regarded within the organisation.

(The digital illusion takes shape, spreading like wildfire through the digital channels. False rumours of Desdemona and Cassio's secret affair begin to surface.)

(Describing the spreading illusion) The digital realm, once a place of order, now trembles with rumours and deception. The lines between truth and falsehood blur, and Othello's trust hangs in the balance.

(As the false rumours reach Othello's ears, the once-unwavering trust in Desdemona starts to crumble.)

OTHELLO: (with a furrowed brow.) Desdemona, have you been talking to Cassio?

DESDEMONA: (*confused*) Cassio? No, not recently. Why do you ask?

OTHELLO: (*torn*) I've heard things, Desdemona. Rumours.

(The tension in the office escalates as Othello confronts Desdemona, their virtual world disrupted by the shadows of suspicion.)

DESDEMONA: (hurt and bewildered) Othello, I don't understand. What rumours?

OTHELLO: (struggling with his emotions) they say... They say you and Cassio are having an affair.

SCENE 3

(The stage transitions to a high-tech, minimalist apartment. Desdemona sits at her sleek computer desk, engrossed in a virtual conversation with Cassio. Othello, in another corner of the room, watches their interaction with growing suspicion and anguish.)

NARRATOR: (Setting the scene) The digital age has extended its reach into personal spaces. In a sleek, minimalist apartment, Desdemona engages in a virtual conversation, unaware of Othello's watchful eyes. Othello, consumed by doubt, observes their interaction, his heart heavy with suspicion.

DESDEMONA: (animated, typing) Cassio, it's been a while since we caught up. How's everything on your end?

CASSIO: (Charming, virtual) Desdemona, it is always a pleasure to chat with you. Things are good, but I miss our in-person meetings. The virtual world can only capture so much.

(As Desdemona and Cassio exchange pleasantries in the digital realm, Othello's growing suspicion tightens its grip.)

OTHELLO: (muttering to himself) Cassio... Desdemona... What's the nature of their virtual meetings?

(Desdemona continues her conversation with Cassio, the words on her screen painting a picture of camaraderie and friendship.)

DESDEMONA: (virtual smile) I agree, Cassio. The virtual world lacks the warmth of a face-to face conversation. But it's convenient for now, given our busy schedules.

CASSIO: (virtual laughter) True, true. Speaking of convenience, have you considered our little project? I think it's time we put our heads together.

(The mention of their "project" raises Othello's suspicion to new heights. He approaches Desdemona.)

OTHELLO: (tense) Desdemona, what project is he talking about?

DESDEMONA: (started) Othello! I didn't realise you were listening. It's a work-related project, nothing more.

(The tension in the room is palpable as Othello's doubts intensify.)

OTHELLO: (Accusingly) work-related, you say? Your conversations with him seem rather personal.

DESDEMONA: (defensive) Othello, you're reading too much into it. Cassio and I have always collaborated closely.

(In the digital age, trust can be shattered by a single message. Othello's mind races, torn between his love for Desdemona and the web of suspicion.)

OTHELLO: (agitated) Desdemona, I can't help but wonder if there's more to this than meets the eye. I thought our bond was unbreakable.

DESDEMONA: (desperate) Othello, please believe me. There's nothing between Cassio and me except friendship and professional collaboration.

(As their conversation escalates, the room seems to shrink around them, the weight of technology pressing in.)

NARRATOR: (observing the digital battlefield) In the confines of this modern apartment, trust unravels like a thread pulled from a sweater.

Othello, trapped in a web of suspicion, questions the very foundation of his relationship with Desdemona.

CASSIO: (virtual concern) Desdemona, I never meant to cause any trouble. If my messages make you uncomfortable, I'll back off.

DESDEMONA: (torn) No, Cassio, it's not your fault. It's just a misunderstanding.

(Unbeknownst to Desdemona, Othello's anguish deepens as he watches her defend her virtual relationship with Cassio.)

OTHELLO: (inwardly tortured) How could she defend him like this? Is there something she's not telling me?

(The room grows colder; the digital divide between trust and suspicion widens.)

DESDEMONA: (*virtual sincerity*) Othello, please, let's talk about this calmly when I'm done with my conversation. There's nothing to worry about.

(Desdemona returns to her virtual conversation with Cassio, leaving Othello alone with his turmoil.)

OTHELLO: (*whispering, broken*) Nothing to worry about, but my heart tells me otherwise.

SCENE 4

(The stage is an upscale apartment. Othello and Desdemona are in the midst of a heated argument. Desdemona is emotionally hurt, and Othello is overwhelmed by doubt and anger.)

NARRATOR: (Setting the scene) Amid the digital era, where every word and action can be captured and manipulated, we find ourselves in an upscale apartment. The love that once flourished here is now a battleground of emotions.

DESDEMONA: (Tears in her eyes, her voice trembling.) Othello, I can't believe you would accuse me of such a thing. Our love should be stronger than baseless rumours.

OTHELLO: (torn but resolute) Desdemona, you can't deny the messages and the conversations I saw. They were intimate—too intimate for just colleagues.

(Othello's mind drifts back to that night when he discovered the message.)

NARRATOR: (Flashback) Othello recalls the night he stumbled upon the incriminating message. He was alone in their dimly lit apartment, scrolling through his tablet, when he noticed a notification on Desdemona's device, left carelessly on the coffee table. Curiosity got the best of him, and he opened the message. It was a digital confession of love from Cassio, addressed to Desdemona. The words had seared into his memory.

OTHELLO: (torn, remembering) I was alone, Desdemona, in our apartment. I saw Cassio's message on your device confessing his love for you.

(Their argument reaches a crescendo, and Desdemona, feeling deeply wounded, makes a difficult decision.)

DESDEMONA: (Choked up, grabbing her coat.) I can't do this right now, Othello. I need some space to think.

(Desdemona leaves the apartment, her departure marking a moment of profound silence. Alone and devastated, Othello begins to crumble under the weight of his emotions.)

NARRATOR: (Setting the Stage) As Desdemona's footsteps fade away, the apartment plunges into a heavy silence. Othello, left alone, is on the brink of a breakdown.

(Just then, there is a knock on the door. Iago and Roderigo, pretending to be there on official business, enter the apartment.)

IAGO: (faking surprise) Othello, my apologies for the interruption. We were here to discuss some security matters, but it seems we've walked into something unexpected.

RODERIGO: (feigning concern) Are you all right, Othello?

(Othello, his emotions in turmoil, tries to compose himself. The memory of that fateful night when he stumbled upon the incriminating message haunts him.)

OTHELLO: (forcing a smile) Iago, Roderigo, it's nothing. It was just a personal matter. What brings you here?

Iago: (pretending innocence) We thought this was the designated meeting place. Security matters, you know.

RODERIGO: (nodding) Yes, we didn't mean to intrude, but we can come back later.

OTHELLO: (wiping away a tear) No, no need for that. Let's discuss whatever you came for.

(Othello's recollection deepens the turmoil within him as Iago and Roderigo, aware of his vulnerability, prepare to exploit his doubts.)

OTHELLO: (His voice is quivering.) Iago, Roderigo, I don't know what to do. I saw a message on her device from Cassio, confessing his love for her.

IAGO: (turning to Roderigo with a sly smile) Roderigo, it's an opportune moment. Our dear Othello seems to be in quite a predicament, doesn't he?

RODERIGO: (nodding, whispering) Perfect, Iago. His trust in Desdemona is shattered.

IAGO: (addressing Othello, feigning sympathy) Othello, my friend, this situation is indeed troubling. We should consider our options carefully.

OTHELLO: (Considering) yes, you're right, Iago. I need to sort this out, but I don't know where to begin.

(Roderigo, panicking, steps forward.)

RODERIGO: *(panicking)* Othello, what if she's been deceiving you all along?

(Iago steps in, adopting a tone of reason.)

IAGO: *(innocently)* Let's gather more information, Othello. The truth always reveals itself in the end.

SCENE 5

(The stage is set in Othello and Desdemona's sleek, modern apartment. The digital screens that once radiated warmth now cast an eerie, blue glow. Othello, his face twisted with jealousy and rage, stands near a computer, while Desdemona sits on the couch, her face etched with heartbreak.)

NARRATOR: (Setting the scene) In the heart of their once-happy home, where lines of code once stood as a testament to their shared passion for technology, we find Othello and Desdemona, now estranged, trapped in the shadows of suspicion.

OTHELLO: (accusatory, his voice trembling) Desdemona, I can't ignore it any longer. These messages, these conversations, I've seen...

DESDEMONA: (Desperate, her eyes filling with tears) Othello, please, you have to believe me. I would never betray you.

(Othello's mind flashes back to that night when he stumbled upon the incriminating message.)

NARRATOR: (*Flashback*) Othello recalls the night he discovered the message. Alone in their dimly lit apartment, he was scrolling through his tablet when he noticed a notification on Desdemona's device, left carelessly on the coffee table. Curiosity got the best of him, and he opened the message. It was a digital confession of love from Cassio, addressed to Desdemona. The words had seared into his memory.

OTHELLO: (tormented, remembering) I was alone, Desdemona, in our apartment. I saw Cassio's message on your device confessing his love for you.

(Desdemona, her heart heavy, reaches out to Othello, but he pulls away.)

DESDEMONA: (*Desperate*) Othello, please, you have to believe me. Cassio is a colleague, nothing more.

OTHELLO: (*angry, his voice rising*) Colleague? The messages were more than just professional, Desdemona! They were intimate—too intimate for colleagues!

(The tension in the room thickens as Othello's accusations hang in the air. Desdemona, unable to bear his mistrust, rises from the couch.)

DESDEMONA: (heartbroken, her voice quivering.) If you can't trust me, Othello, I don't know how we can move forward.

(Desdemona exits, leaving Othello alone, his heart heavy with doubt.)

NARRATOR: (Setting the Stage) As Desdemona's footsteps fade away, the apartment plunges into a heavy silence. Othello, left alone, is on the brink of a breakdown.

(Just then, there is a knock on the door. Emilia, Desdemona's loyal friend and Iago's wife, enters the apartment.)

EMILIA: (worried, observing Othello) Othello, Desdemona is in tears. What happened?

OTHELLO: (distraught, his voice breaking) Emilia, I don't know what to believe anymore. I've seen messages, Emilia, that suggest...

EMILIA:(Concerned, connecting the dots) Messages? Othello, it can't be what it seems. Iago, my husband, has been acting strange lately, and I've overheard things. Iago's been up to something sinister.

OTHELLO: (confused, seeking answers) Iago? What does he have to do with this?

(Emilia, now deeply suspicious, starts putting the pieces together.)

EMILIA: (Resolutely) I'm not sure, Othello, but I have a feeling he might be behind all of this. We need to find out the truth.

(As Othello and Emilia exchange worried glances, the realisation dawns that their trust has been shattered and a dark presence lurks behind the scenes.)

SCENE 6

(The stage transitions to Emilia and Iago's apartment, dimly lit with a few screens scattered around. Emilia, determined and suspicious, sits at a computer, typing furiously. Iago, seemingly oblivious, watches TV in the background.)

NARRATOR: (Setting the scene) In the shadows of a digital realm, Emilia, driven by a sense of betrayal, sifts through the fragments of deception that threaten to destroy her friend's life.

EMILIA: (Muttering to herself as she clicks through files) There has to be something here, something that links Iago to this mess.

(Emilia uncovers a series of edited files, revealing the meticulous manipulation behind the scenes. She starts connecting the dots, tracing back to the source of the fabricated messages.)

(Eyes widening with realisation) This... this is a digital trail of deceit. These messages, these files—they've all been tampered with.

(Emilia pulls up a timeline, showing the exact moments when the digital fabrications took place. The evidence points unmistakably to Iago)

NARRATOR:(revealing the truth) The pieces of the puzzle fall into place. Emilia, driven by her loyalty to Desdemona, has uncovered the truth that threatens to shatter Othello's world.

EMILIA: (whispering to herself) Iago, you've been orchestrating this from the start. But why? What could drive you to do this to them?

(Emilia prints out the digital evidence, ready to confront Iago and reveal his sinister plot.)

SCENE 7

(The stage transforms into Othello and Desdemona's apartment, illuminated with a soft, contemplative light. Othello sits on the couch, deep in thought, while Desdemona stands near the window, looking out at the digital cityscape.)

NARRATOR: (Setting the scene) In the aftermath of digital deception, our characters find themselves at a crossroads, grappling with the consequences of technology's manipulation.

(Emilia enters, holding the digital evidence she uncovered in the previous SCENE. Her demeanour is determined.)

EMILIA: (*resolutely*) Othello, Desdemona, there's something you need to see. Iago—he's behind all of this. (Desdemona and Othello turn their attention to Emilia, a mixture of surprise and curiosity in their eyes.)

DESDEMONA: (*surprised*) Emilia, what do you mean? (Emilia explains the evidence she found, showcasing Iago's manipulation.)

EMILIA: (*Firm*) Iago has been weaving a web of deceit, manipulating digital messages, and sowing discord between you two. Look at this—(She shows them the evidence on her tablet)—he orchestrated the entire illusion.

(Othello's anger intensifies, and Desdemona is deeply affected by the revelation.)

OTHELLO: (*Angry*) Iago... I trusted him like a brother. How could he do this to us?

EMILIA: (*Firm*) We can't change the past, but we can expose the truth and prevent others from falling victim to his schemes.

(As they digest the truth and determine their next steps, Othello and Desdemona share a moment of reconciliation.)

DESDEMONA: (*softly*) Othello, I never imagined our love would be tested like this. It's as if we were puppets in someone else's digital theatre.

OTHELLO: (*Regretful*) Desdemona, I let my doubts and jealousy cloud my judgement. I doubted you, and for that, I can never forgive myself.

(Desdemona moves closer to Othello, their bond slowly mending.)

DESDEMONA: (Touched) Othello, we're both victims of this digital age. It's easy to lose sight of the truth when everything can be manipulated. But I never stopped loving you.

OTHELLO: (apologetic) And I never stopped loving you, Desdemona. Can you find it in your heart to forgive me?

(Desdemona reaches out, and they embrace, which symbolises their reconciliation.)

NARRATOR: (reflecting) Love prevails in the heart of the digital storm. Othello and Desdemona find solace in each other; their love is rekindled through the trials of deception.

(Together, they decide to confront Iago and reveal his actions to their colleagues, vowing to stand against digital deception.)

(concluding) In the wake of deception, our characters emerge stronger, their bonds forged by the trials of the digital age. As they unite to expose Iago, they become advocates for digital literacy and ethics, ensuring that truth prevails in the age of technology.

(Desdemona, Othello, and Emilia share a moment of unity and purpose. The SCENE expands to show their discussions and preparations, allowing the audience to witness their determination and resolve. As they plan their next steps, the lights slowly dim, leaving the audience with a sense of resolution and hope).

XVIII
THE TRAGEDY OF EDWARD - VAIBHAV ARORA

SCENE 1

(The Royal Court. A lavishly decorated chamber in the Danish Castle, dimly lit by Candlelight. King Edward sits on his throne. The Queen, adorned in opulent garments, stands beside him.)

(Robin, Edward's brother, enters and the three characters engage in a tense conversation.)

KING EDWARD: (With a weary expression) My dear Mary, I have noticed your growing fascination with materialistic things and power.

QUEEN MARY: (Feigning innocence) My love, I only wish to see our kingdom prosper and thrive under your rule.

ROBIN: (Whispering to Mary) Mary, we must proceed with our plan. I cannot bear to see you suffer in this marriage any longer.

QUEEN MARY: (Gazing at Robin) My heart belongs to you, Robin. We must act swiftly.

KING EDWARD: (Suspicious) What secrets do you two share?

ROBIN: (Nervous) Secrets, brother? None at all.

QUEEN MARY: (Smiling sweetly) We merely speak of our love for this kingdom and your wisdom, dear Edward.

(A dimly lit room. Mary stands by a table with a glass of water. Edward and William are seated nearby.)

QUEEN MARY: (Whispering to herself) This is it. Edward won't see it coming.

(Edward enters and approaches the table.)

KING EDWARD: Mary, could I have some water, please?

QUEEN MARY: Of course, Edward. (Pours the poison into the glass)

(Just as Edward reaches for the glass, Courtier James enters and takes the glass instead.)

JAMES: (Taking a sip) Ah, thank you, Mary. I was quite thirsty.

KING EDWARD: (Panicking) No, wait!

(James suddenly collapses.)

WILLIAM: (Shocked) What just happened?

QUEEN MARY: (Stuttering)I... I don't know! It was meant for Edward!

(James lies motionless on the floor.)

(The royal chamber in Denmark. Mary and Robin are seated, while William enters.)

WILLIAM: (Angrily) Mother! Uncle Robin!

QUEEN MARY: (Startled) William, you're back!

ROBIN: (Nervously) It's been a while, my boy.

WILLIAM: (Accusingly)I can't believe what I've heard. You two were behind Father's death?

QUEEN MARY: (Defensively) William, it's not what you think.

WILLIAM: (Furious)Don't lie to me, Mother!

(William storms out of the room.)

(In another SCENE, William is speaking with a trusted confidant.)

CONFIDANT: William, you look deeply troubled. What's happened?

WILLIAM: (Tearfully)I've learned the truth about my father's death. My own mother and uncle conspired to kill him.

CONFIDANT: (Incredulous)Unthinkable! What are you going to do?

WILLIAM: (Resolute)I can't let them get away with this. I must seek justice for my father.

SCENE 2

(A quiet, sombre evening by the riverbank. William sits alone, lost in thought.)

WILLIAM: (Whispers to himself) I can't believe she's gone too. The Courtier's Daughter... She couldn't bear the pain of losing her father, James.

(As he speaks, a shadowy figure appears.)

(William turns to see a ghostly apparition of the Courtier's Daughter.)

WILLIAM: (Startled)You...you're here?

COURTIER'S DAUGHTER'S GHOST: (Sorrowful) I couldn't go on without my father. The grief was too much.

WILLIAM: (Tears in his eyes) And now, I've lost you as well.

COURTIER'S DAUGHTER'S GHOST: (Whispers)We're both trapped in this endless sorrow.

(They share a moment of silent sadness by the river, two souls weighed down by their losses).

(A dimly lit chamber in the castle. Mary and Robin stand facing each other.)

QUEEN MARY: (Frustrated)Robin, you've pushed me too far! I won't be treated like this anymore.

ROBIN: (Defiant)Mary, you're obsessed with power. It's tearing us apart.

QUEEN MARY: (Plotting)Power is everything, Robin.

QUEEN MARY: (Whispers to the soldiers) It's time to execute the plan. Get rid of Robin.

(Robin's murder takes place, and Mary ascends the throne.)

(The throne rooms. Mary, now Queen, addresses her subjects.)

QUEEN MARY: (Confident) Today, I assume the throne.

SCENE 3

(A hidden chamber deep within the castle. William confronts his mother Mary, who is seated with a sinister air.)

(William draws his sword, and Mary stands, drawing her own.)

WILLIAM: (Determined) I'll do what's necessary to end your reign of terror.

(A tense sword fight ensues, echoing through the chamber. Mary and William clash with ferocity.)

WILLIAM: Your reign of terror ends now!

(William disarms his mother Mary and strikes her down.)

(William stands alone, heavy-hearted but resolved.)

(The grand hall of the palace. William, crowned as King, addresses his subjects.)

WILLIAM: (Addressing the crowd) My fellow subjects, today marks the beginning of a new era for Denmark.

(With determination) My people, I accept the responsibility of kingship with a promise – integrity and justice shall be our guiding lights.

SUBJECTS: (Nodding approvingly) Hear, hear!

WILLIAM: No more shall manipulation and greed poison our land. Together, we will build a kingdom founded on principles of fairness and compassion.

SUBJECTS: (With enthusiasm) Long live King William! (Cheering)Hail the new era!

(Exit)

XIX

LOYALTY AND LOSS: A TITUS TALE - VALLENTINA V

SCENE 1

(Rome's best champion, Andronicus returns with honour and prosperity, from where he drew a bound sword and subjected Rome's enemy to rule.)

(Tamora and her sons are restrained. Martius and Quintus arrive. Aaron is followed by other inmates, goths, and military personnel)

TITUS ANDRONICUS: Hail to Rome, conqueror of the weeping weeds!

Bringing priceless jading back to the bay.

Andronicus arrives, bound by laurel boughs. To re-salute his nation with tears of genuine gladness for his return to Rome.

Show respect for the ceremonies we have planned!

Rome will shower those who survive with affection;

These I convey to their most recent residence, where they will be buried with their ancestors:

I have permission from the Goths to put away my blade here.

Titus, heedless and cruel to thyself.

LUCIUS: Lord, give me one of the prisoners, I shall cut their limbs and they will never raise against our Roman empire again.

TITUS ANDRONICUS: I offer him, the eldest son of this distraught queen. One of the noblest survivors.

TAMORA: Halt! You shall not go near my son.

Glorious Titus, the tears I shed are the mother's tears of passion for her son.

My son is innocent, we were captured and brought to Rome. To beautify thy triumphs and return, why do my sons be killed? The great Andronicus, do not stain your hands with our blood, We beg to show your mercy on us. Please, don't hurt my firstborn.

TITUS ANDRONICUS: Please pardon me and have patience, ma'am. These are customs we follow.

Goths were defeated and your son must die as a result of their request for a sacrifice.

TAMORA: Oh cruel, irreligious piety

TITUS ANDRONICUS: Oh, let it be so, let them serve us in our palace and make this a last farewell to your son's soul, in peace and honour.

(Kills Alarbus)

(Exeunt)

(Entry in palace with Titus Andronicus and the prisoners)

CAPTAIN: Oh, great lord, the judgement is going to begin.

TITUS ANDRONICUS: It shall be done, take them (*Titus entering the court*)

QUINTUS & MARTIUS: Lord! My father! The false accusation is what made me stand here in front of you.

We are innocents. We want nothing but good for our country, and for us!

CAPTAIN: You opposed our rules and worked against Rome!

MARTIUS: We (Titus interrupts the captain)

could never go against the rules and we would never want any harm to our people!

QUINTUS: Yes, my lord. This is a completely false accusation levelled at us. There is someone who wants us to be killed by your hands. They wanted your son's blood on your hand.

MARTIUS: There is no such evidence against us.

CAPTAIN: Oh, the evidence is there. Why did you—

TITUS ANDRONICUS: Enough! I believe my son's. This is a false accusation. And they shall be released and they'll stand by my side for the rest of the wars. They'll be the head of the empire.

(Enter Lavina)

LAVINA: May you live in peace and honour Lord Titus, my noble Lord and father.

For your return to Rome, shed on the earth.

Oh, grant me this place with your triumphant hand, whose fortunes Rome's finest citizen's cheer.

TITUS ANDRONICUS: Kind Rome, that has my cordial and to cheer my heart, with a lovingly reserved.

Lavinia is eternal, surpassing even the days of thy father and renowned for her virtues!

(Enter Saturnius)

TITUS ANDRONICUS: Hail the great Titus! Who won a long battle with Goth's and brought their queen and her sons.

(Enter Lucius)

SATURNIUS: Pay close attention, honourable patricians who support my rights.

Being his firstborn son and the last to wear Rome's imperial diadem, I continue to carry my father's honours.

TITUS ANDRONICUS: Prince Saturninus, patience.

SATURNIUS: Do me right, Romans.

Sheathe and draw your swords, patriots.

Until I be the emperor of Rome, Saturninus.

Titus have killed people and you shall go to hell, I would rather be here robbing people's hearts.

LUCIUS: Proud Saturninus. But I shall be the next emperor.

TITUS ANDRONICUS: Prince, be content with yourself.

I'll give you back the hearts of the people and wean them off of themselves.

The next emperor would be Prince Saturninus and Lucius you would praise him as thee.

SATURNIUS: Titus Andronicus, for my favours are done.

The royal mistress of Rome Lavinia will become my empress in order to further that honourable family name. Would you accept this?

TITUS ANDRONICUS: Indeed, honourable lord. I consider myself extremely honoured for your grace in this match.

SATURNIUS: I'm grateful, father of my life, noble Titus.

I'm so proud of you and your gifts.

LUCIUS: I must not accept this! Lavinia gets wed to Saturninus? No, my lord, I should be the next Rome emperor.

SATURNIUS: My people and your father have already made their decision. (He whispers in Lucius's ears) I shall rule the Rome and you shall not be there to see it, Lucius. (He fakes getting hit by Lucius)

O Lord of heavens! He attempted to hurt me! How this is even permitted? God Almighty! I'm hurting!

LUCIUS: I never made contact with you. He— (gets interrupted by his shouting)

SATURNIUS: You shall leave this kingdom and never enter.

Soldiers! Take him far away. He shall never come back.

LUCIUS: No one can touch me. I will leave but I will come back.

This is my kingdom and I will return.

(Exeunt)

SCENE 2

(Saturninus meets Lavinia in the garden while Tamora & Aaron watching them)

SATURNIUS: Hail the most beautiful lady in Rome and soon to be my empress. The moon and sky are far less beautiful than you.

LAVINA: O my lord, your words are as sweet as the finest nectar, and your compliments fill my heart with joy.

SATURNIUS: I would kiss you and then go to hell if I could, just to tell the devil that I saw heaven without actually going there.

LAVINA: I shall be pleased my prince but it sh——

(Lavinia hears someone calling Saturninus)

SATURNIUS: Okay princess, I shall see you to-morrow then. Allow your neighbours to come outside and listen to the rich music as it reveals the imagined happiness that each of them has received from their encounters.

(He kisses her and leaves the place)

TAMORA: They shall be redeemed for what they have done to us. Oh! My veins burn from anger.

AARON: Calm down my lady, to do some fatal execution?

We shall take our revenge and take over Rome to save the Goths.

TAMORA: Conquer Rome? Ha! That isn't feasible given our current situation.

We have to cause destruction. He killed my dearest son.

AARON: We'll definitely cause his downfall. My mind is pounding with blood and revenge; I have death in my hand and vengeance in my heart.

To avenge your son's murder we will harm Lavinia, Titus' beautiful daughter!

TAMORA: What? Execute Lavinia.

AARON: Yes, my lord, we will kill Lavinia.

(Enter Chiron, Demetrius)

CHIRON & DEMETRIUS: No, not murder. We must take action beyond simply killing her.

DEMETRIUS: She and her father should suffer. Her death should be brutal.

AARON: I have a plan to make them suffer. Do as I say.

DEMETRIUS & CHIRON: Yes, my lord.

(Exeunt)

SCENE 3

(Lavinia is sitting alone after she met Saturninus)

LAVINA: O how lovely it is to see the moon. The beauty is yet to be discovered in your serene glow and the glistening face illuminates the night with beauty and colour.

(Enter Demetrius and Chiron)

DEMETRIUS: Now would be the ideal moment to murder her, Chiron. They will be held accountable for everything they have done to our brother and our Kingdom!

CHIRON: Yes, my brother! We shall get back at them.

(They attempt to kill Lavina)

CAPTAIN: Empress watch out! (Lavinia escapes the sword)

LAVINA: Soldiers. Who are you? How did you enter the palace?

(Demetrius & Chiron runs away while soldiers were behind them)

CAPTAIN: Empress, are you okay? We shall catch him, my lord.

LAVINA: Go find out who it was and bring them back to my father.

Inform him that there are enemies inside the palace.

(Demetrius & Chiron escapes the soldiers and they met the queen)

DEMETRIUS: The foolish captain intervened to save the empress just as we were about to kill her!

TAMORA: Fair and foul deeds go hand in hand. Fate stopped the act of taking a life. The target survived, but the darkness continued to grow.

CHIRON: Don't worry mother, she shall die in our hands.

AARON: Have patience my lady, I have a different idea that would work this time.

(Exeunt)

(Titus's palace)

TITUS ANDRONICUS: Someone tried killing my daughter. I wouldn't spare their lives. I shall execute them.

SATURNIUS: They shall pay for what they have done. Captain, did you find out who it was?

CAPTAIN: Not yet my lord, but there is a messenger who wants to talk with you.

(A messenger enters)

MESSENGER: Greetings my lord Titus Andronicus and Prince Saturninus. I have some news to share.

TITUS ANDRONICUS: Is it?

MESSENGER: While I was passing by the prisoner's rooms, I overheard Tomora and Aaron discussing their plans to assassinate, but they were not successful.

(Messenger exits)

TITUS: They attempted to murder my daughter? They will have to pay for it!

(Exeunt)

SCENE 4

(Titus's palace, a banquet set out, Saturninus is unaware of Titus executing Tamora sons)

TITUS ANDRONICUS: Welcome, fearsome queen; welcome, my gracious lords. Greetings, emperor, warlike Goths, and everyone else. Despite the low spirits, please eat until it fills your bellies.

BASSIANUS: Lord Titus Andronicus, what a delightful surprise.

SATURNIUS: Why are you dressed like this, Andronicus?

TITUS ANDRONICUS: Since I would make sure everything was in order to host your empress and your highness.

TAMORA: We are honoured for this meal my lord, but where are my sons? It's been a while since I saw them. My lord did you witness them?

AARON: Last I saw them they were near the garden. Have they not come to meet you?

TITUS ANDRONICUS: They are both baked in that pie, which their mother has fed delightfully, consuming the flesh that she has bred.

TAMORA: The pie which I just ate is my son's. How cruel you can be?

TITUS ANDRONICUS: It's true, witness the sharpness of my knife.

(Titus ends Tamora's life by slashing her throat)

AARON: My Lady! Titus Andronicus. First you baked my sons into a pie and then you killed the love of my life. I will not spare you!

(Aaron takes a sword and stabs Lavinia and escapes)

SATURNIUS: Look what have you done Titus. Your deeds will be the cause of your daughter's death.

TITUS ANDRONICUS: My deeds? Oh, it shall— (gets interprets by Bassianus)

BASSIANUS: He may be to blame but you are responsible too Saturnius. Without an empress there shall be no emperor.

(Kills Saturninus)

BASSIANUS: Lord forgives me for murdering my own brother. It had to be done. The Throne is mine now.

(Exeunt)

SCENE 5

(Aaron is been found out by soldiers)

TITUS ANDRONICUS: Immerse him up to his chest in the ground and chop off his hands, he shall starve to death. Allow him to stand, rave, and cry out for food.

AARON: I should be sorry for the evils I did. I did ten thousand things worse than before, but still I —

TITUS ANDRONICUS: You shall die in pain!

(Exeunt)

(Enter Lucius along with Goths army)

LUCIUS: Where is he? Saturnious come out and defeat me now!

BASSIANUS: Oh Lucius, you are still alive? I thought you were long dead.

LUCIUS: Where is the emperor?

BASSIANUS: O you're looking at him! I am the emperor. Rome is mine.

LUCIUS: Not when I am still alive. I shall be the next emperor.

HA! You the emperor of the almighty Rome? Save this child, O Lord!

BASSIANUS: Have you lost your way Lucius? Without your dad, the almighty Titus Andronicus. You are nothing, just nothing, almighty you say. You and your father are insignificant in front of me. I shall kill you first and then your father. I will reign as Rome's sole emperor.

LUCIUS: You the emperor? You killed your own brother for this throne. Bassianus, the late emperor, would never have done anything like this.

Spare your life and run far away Bassianus, my father is ruthless. Before that you might be slaughtered by the people of Rome.

BASSIANUS: Rome is mine Lucius. It belongs to my father. I have the full authority and you will perish at my hands.

TITUS ANDRONICUS: You can't kill my son when I'm still alive, Bassianus. You have no right to rule over Rome when you have your brother's blood in your hand.

LUCIUS: No, my lord, I shall kill him at my own cost. He shall die in my arms.

(Lucius and Bassianus draw their sword and start fighting. Lucius kills Bassianus by stabbing him)

TITUS ANDRONICUS: My son, my blood! You have rescued our people and triumphed over Bassianus. You will rule Rome as our next emperor.

LUCIUS: Atlas the kingdom is mine!

(Exeunt)

XX
UNRAVELLING HEARTS - VARUN YUNAS

SCENE 1

(At Baptista's house, Enter Baptista and Katherine)

BAPTISTA: You need to start thinking about getting settled. You have reached the age where you should be getting married.

KATHERINE: But I can't be marrying just anyone, right? Shouldn't I also be in love with that person?

BAPTISTA: You can fall in love after getting married, can't you?

KATHERINE: What kind of logic is that, Father?

BAPTISTA: Trust me, my child. This is not as uncommon as you think it is. I even have a boy in my mind for you.

KATHERINE: Oh please, don't start with this again, Father.

BAPTISTA: Listen to me once. His name is Petruchio and he is new in town and he wants to take you as his wife.

KATHERINE: He hasn't even met me once; how can he want to get married right away?

BAPTISTA: That is not going to be an issue. I have invited him over for lunch today so go put on your best clothes and keep an extra plate on the dining table.

(Enter Bianca)

BIANCA: I hear a boy is coming for lunch. What is that?

BAPTISTA: His name is Petruchio and he is coming to see your sister.

BIANCA: Wow. (To Katherine) You have to present yourself to him in the best possible light, or else you will never get married, while I myself haven't tied the knot yet.

KATHERINE: Oh, shut up, Bianca!

BAPTISTA: Well, she is not wrong. You should really take this opportunity seriously. You won't find many better men than him; he is a good man.

BIANCA: Yeah, Father's right. Don't just blow him off. At least give him a chance.

KATHERINE: I will think about it.

(Katherine and Bianca Exits)

(Enter Petruchio)

BAPTISTA: Well, look who we have here. Welcome, welcome Petruchio.

PETRUCHIO: Thank you, Sir.

BAPTISTA: I hope you didn't have a hard time finding our home?

PETRUCHIO: No Sir, absolutely no trouble finding a place this big. (*Looking around*) I must say you have a lovely home.

BAPTISTA: Well, thank you. I won't take up much of your time. Go meet the person you came for. (Going to the stairs and calling Katherine) Katherine dear, come and meet our guest.

KATHERINE: (From inside her room)Yes Father, coming. Give me one second.

(Enter Katherine as she climbs down the stairs wearing a very pretty gown)

BAPTISTA: What a beautiful daughter I have. Petruchio is definitely going to fall for you.

KATHERINE: Oh, don't say such things.

(Katherine and Baptista make their way towards Petruchio)

BAPTISTA:(To Petruchio) Here, this is my daughter, Katherine (To Katherine) and this young gentleman here is Petruchio.

PETRUCHIO: It is my pleasure to meet you, Miss Katherine. (Takes her hand gently) You look lovely today (Kisses her hand).

KATHERINE: Why, thank you so much. It is nice to meet you too.

BAPTISTA: Come, no need to stand and talk. Sit. (All three sitting on chairs) So, Petruchio, tell us more about yourself. Where you are from and what do you do for a living?

PETRUCHIO: I am originally from Wessex but I have recently moved to the town of Padua. I am a merchant and I moved here in hopes to increase my trade.

BAPTISTA: Very well. Now, let me ask you. What are your thoughts on my daughter, Katherine?

PETRUCHIO: (*chuckles*) I see you dislike wasting time and prefer to get right to the point.

BAPTISTA: I have never been a beating around the bush kind of guy.

PETRUCHIO: Well, I really like your daughter and even though I am seeing her for the first time I would love to marry her.

KATHERINE: How can you want to marry me if you don't love me?

PETRUCHIO: I do, however, like you. People have told me that you are a strong and independent woman, which are qualities that would entice any suitor. You and I aren't getting any younger, and you know how this society works; it'll just keep getting on our nerves until we get married.

KATHERINE: Those were some nice words. You know what, I'll think about your proposal.

PETRUCHIO: Thank you for considering. Now, I don't want to overstay my welcome. I will be taking my leave. Good day!

(Petruchio Exits)

BAPTISTA: He left in a hurry. So, Katherine, how did you feel about him? Did you find him appealing?

KATHERINE: I might be open to the idea of him as a husband.

BAPTISTA: Wow, that's great news. *(loudly)* Bianca, come on in here.

(Enter Bianca)

BIANCA: What happened, Father?

BAPTISTA: Your sister is willing to marry the guy who came today.

BIANCA: That is fantastic news. At least, she won't end up alone her whole life.

KATHERINE: Oh, shut up you guys!

SCENE 2

(The day of Petruchio and Katherine's wedding. At the wedding chapel. Enter Katherine and Bianca.)

BIANCA: You look lovely, my dear sister.

KATHERINE: Thank you so much, Bianca.

BIANCA: Look, here comes Father.

(Enter Baptista)

BAPTISTA:*(tense)* There she is my lovely daughter. You look beautiful, Katherine.

KATHERINE: Thank you, Father.

BAPTISTA: You are not having second thoughts about the wedding, right?

KATHERINE: (chuckles)No, Father. I am sure about my decision to get married.

BAPTISTA: Good. I am so proud of you.

KATHERINE: Thank you, Father. But why do you look so tense?

BAPTISTA: That is because we have a bit of a situation here. Your soon to be husband still hasn't arrived for his own wedding. His friends have gone to look for him and I am sure they will find him.

KATHERINE: *(Having a breakdown)* What if he ran away? What if he leaves me standing at the altar?

BAPTISTA: I am sure it's nothing like that. I am sure he will be here any minute. Maybe his car broke down or something.

KATHERINE: *(In tears)* This is why I refused to get married until now. I don't deserve such happiness. I will stay with you and take care of you in your old age.

(Enter Petruchio's friend)

PETRUCHIO'S FRIEND: Petruchio has reached the chapel. We found him at his house. He woke up late.

BAPTISTA: Good, now we can start the ceremony.

(Petruchio's friend Exits)

KATHERINE: (Wiping her tears)Thank God, he is here.

BAPTISTA: So, you're telling me you're not nervous about your wedding? Listen, there is no one else more deserving of happiness than you. Now, let's get out there.

(The ceremony begins as Baptista walks Katherine down the aisle with Petruchio looking at his would-be bride in awe)

BAPTISTA:(giving away Katherine to Petruchio)Now, you take care of my little girl and never break her heart.

PETRUCHIO: (still in awe of Katherine's beauty) Yes, sir.

(The ceremony begins.)

CELEBRANT: Now, I believe you have your vows with you.

PETRUCHIO: I didn't really prepare the vows, so I'll just say what comes to mind. I, Petruchio, take you, Katherine, as my legally married wife. I promise to support you through all of life's ups and downs and to assist you in your future endeavours.

(Puts a ring on Katherine's finger)

CELEBRANT: (looking towards Katherine) Now you.

KATHERINE: Yes. I, Katherine, take you, Petruchio, as my lawfully married husband, from this day forward, for better or for worse, richer or poorer, in sickness and in health, until death do us part.

(Puts a ring around Petruchio's finger)

CELEBRANT: Now, I pronounce thee to be husband and wife.

(The ceremony gets over and Katherine is saying her goodbyes)

BIANCA: (Hugging Katherine) I will miss you, sis. I really didn't think that you would get married but here you are. I love you and keep visiting.

KATHERINE: I love you too, Bianca. Take care of yourself.

BAPTISTA: The world out there is rough. I have raised you well and I have protected you to the best of my ability. If I ever failed you, I am really sorry about it. When you leave, always take care of yourself. I love you; you know that. (To Petruchio) Please take care of my little girl.

KATHERINE:*(in tears)* You have been the greatest of fathers. Thank you so much for raising me into such a strong and independent girl. I love you too, Father.

Petruchio: You can always count on me to protect your daughter from now on, sir.

BAPTISTA: That's good to hear. Now, good luck to both of you as you embark on this journey. It won't be the easiest journey, but I'm confident you two will make it through. Goodbye.

(Petruchio and Katherine Exits)

SCENE 3

(At Petruchio and Katherine's house some days after their marriage. Enter Katherine)

KATHERINE: Petruchio! Did you bring the groceries I asked you for?

(Enter Petruchio)

PETRUCHIO: (Waking up from a nap) I am sorry Kat darling; I must have forgotten. I will get you those groceries later today.

KATHERINE: Please stop forgetting such small things. This is not the first time that you forgot to bring the groceries. You even forgot to wake up on time for your own wedding.

PETRUCHIO: And you will never let me forget that, will you?

KATHERINE: Why should I? It was the day of your marriage. It happens once in every person's life. That is one day when I will expect a person to remember to wake up on time.

PETRUCHIO: Again, I am really sorry to scare you like that. Now, I will go and get the groceries you need.

(Petruchio Exits and Enters again after sometime with the groceries)

PETRUCHIO: Here, I got the groceries you needed.

KATHERINE: Thank you for that. (Touching her forehead) I haven't been feeling well today.

PETRUCHIO: (looking concerned)Are you alright? Are you coming down with a cold?

KATHERINE: (her face getting red)Yeah, it could be that.

PETRUCHIO: Why don't you go lie down and take some rest. Let me handle the household chores.: Are you sure about that? I would feel bad about ruining your day off.

PETRUCHIO: (guiding her to the bedroom) You should not worry about such things. You should just take care of your health.

KATHERINE: (lying down on the bed) Okay. If you need anything, ask for my help.

PETRUCHIO: (Puts his fingers on her lips) Shush and go to sleep. Don't worry about all that.

(Petruchio retires Katherine to her bedroom. While she is taking some rest, he proceeds with the household chores.)

PETRUCHIO:(wiping his sweat off) (to himself) I had no idea she did so much every day. I really need to show her more gratitude.

(Petruchio finishes up with the chores. He goes to check up on Katherine. He sees her lying down looking beautiful as ever. Katherine opens her eyes)

KATHERINE: What happened, Petruchio? Is something wrong?

PETRUCHIO: No, nothing like that. How are you feeling now, darling?

KATHERINE: I am feeling much better now. (Getting up from the bed) I think I will go and get dinner ready.

PETRUCHIO: There's no need for that. I've already prepared dinner. You get back into your bed, and I'll bring you dinner.

KATHERINE: But there was no need for that. It was just a flu.

PETRUCHIO: I know it was just a flu, but you should consider it as a holiday for yourself. I had never realized that you did so much for running this house.

KATHERINE: Well, it's not much.

PETRUCHIO: No, it is. And I really need to improve myself to be more worthy of you.

KATHERINE: Don't be so hard on yourself, dear.

PETRUCHIO: I am compelled to. I know I don't show much affection but I love you a lot and mean that. I need to be more grateful to you, and I need to keep my marriage vows by giving you my full support.

KATHERINE: *(blushing)* This means a lot to me. And I may not show it as well but I love you a lot as well. I love how kind you are. And I will do my best to be the wife you desire me to be.

PETRUCHIO: You already are what I always dreamt of.(He leans forward and gives Katherine a peck on her lips) Now, let's have our dinner.

(Petruchio brings the dinner to the bedroom)

KATHERINE: Now, let me see what you've prepared for me on this lovely day.

PETRUCHIO: I have made you your favourite.

KATHERINE: Mushroom Stew?!

PETRUCHIO: Yes, I have.

KATHERINE: Let me try! Let me try!

(Petruchio hands her a bowl of stew. Katherine takes a sip from it)

KATHERINE: (smiling brightly) It is really delicious.

PETRUCHIO:(chuckles) It is, isn't it?

SCENE 4

(At Bianca's wedding ceremony. Enter Petruchio and Katherine.)

PETRUCHIO: The ceremony was lovely, as were the arrangements and other details. What are your thoughts?

KATHERINE: Yes. Yes, it was a nice ceremony.(With a smile on her face)Well, at least the groom came on time.

PETRUCHIO: Would you please let that slide now?

KATHERINE:(laughs) Yeah?

(Enter Baptista)

BAPTISTA: Well, well. You two appear to be in good spirits. How has been life treating you recently?

PETRUCHIO: It has been treating us really well. What do you say, Katherine?

KATHERINE: Well, I must agree it has been treating us well.

BAPTISTA: Petruchio, would you mind getting us some drinks?

PETRUCHIO: Yeah, sure.

(Petruchio exits)

BAPTISTA: So, how is your marriage going, my dear daughter?

KATHERINE: It's been fantastic, Father. I'm so glad I didn't say no to his proposal.

BAPTISTA: I am delighted to hear that you are pleased with him. Before meeting Petruchio, I recall you finding the logic of falling in love after getting married absurd. Do you still believe that?

KATHERINE:(*smiles*) Absolutely not, Father. I believe you now. There hasn't been a single time when I've regretted marrying Petruchio. And, despite the fact that I didn't love him at first, I now adore him.

BAPTISTA: You couldn't have given me a better answer.

(Enter Petruchio)

PETRUCHIO: Here you are. (Hands the drinks to Katherine and Baptista)

KATHERINE: Let's go and see my sister.

(Enter Bianca)

KATHERINE: (hugging Bianca) Congratulations on your big day, Bianca dear. You look gorgeous.

BIANCA: Thank you so much, Kat.

(Bianca Exits)

PETRUCHIO: You yourself look gorgeous.(Takes Katherine's hands)

KATHERINE: (blushing) Do I?

PETRUCHIO: (smiling) Yes, you do.

(They dance to the slow rhythm of the music as Petruchio leans forward and gives a peck on Katherine's lips and they live happily ever after.)

XXI

IN PURSUIT OF REDEMPTION - JASMINE TASING

SCENE 1

(Enter Duke Solinus, Egeon, Gaoler, Officers, and other Attendants in a hall in Duke Solinus' palace)

EGEON: Proceed to end my life in the name of punishment, Solinus.

DUKE SOLINUS: Merchant of Syracuse, plead no longer; I am not fond of breaking our laws: enmity and discord are the true causes of your impending death. If you do not get executed today, it will not be considered fair for our ancestors who fought for Ephesus. And you know what the law says: If anyone born in Ephesus is ever seen at any Syracusian place, death is the answer and similarly the same rule applies here in Ephesus. If I let you go today, it will be unfair for those punished before you. The law, therefore, obliges me and everyone in this court to agree to kill you.

EGEON: I understand what you're saying, but I came here for one reason and one reason only. I knew it would be the cause of my death, but no one understands how critical it is more than I do. Allow me to do this one thing, and then you, My Lord, are free to do whatever you want with me.

DUKE SOLINUS: Well, Syracusan, tell me then. What is this "important" reason for which you put your foot onto the land of my people

EGEON: A more difficult task could not have been imposed, then me talking about my inexpressible griefs. I'll utter what my sorrow gives me permission to leave. I was born in Syracuse, and I married a woman who was happy except for me, had our fortune not been bad. I lived in bliss after she entered my life. Our wealth grew, and I went on successful journeys to Epidamium, which was deadly for me and my family. My wife gave birth to a set of twins, beautiful boys but I lost one of them and his caretaker during the voyage in the sea. We were devastated. My wife left me and my son is not the same. The caretaker too had a twin brother. Nothing has been the same since and after many years I got a notice that my son that I lost and his caretaker might be in this town.

Now my other son and his caretaker left home and came here to look for their twins. So, without considering the consequences, I came forward to find and reunite my family. This is my reason for visiting your property.

DUKE SOLINUS: You are a brave one my friend. Ready to lose your life for your family. I won't lie, I'm impressed and a little moved. But you know I can't justify your punishment, right?

EGEON: Yes, My Lord, I am certain of that, but please allow me to try to locate my son and his companion just once. Whatever the outcome, I'll get back to you so you can move forward with the execution. This is my sole request and assurance to you.

DUKE SOLINUS: Well, Syracusian, you can go find your son. And for your braveness, I'll excuse your life on one condition: if you are successful in finding your son within three weeks, I will let you, your son and his companion go back to Syracuse without any trouble. If the entire court agrees.

GAOLER, OFFICERS AND ATTENDANTS: Yes, My Lord, your decision is the final!

DUKE SOLINUS: Well then dear Syracuse, you are free to find your son. I hope you find him; if not, death is your only option.

EGEON: My Lord, I will forever be grateful for your caring soul.

(Exit Lord Solinus, Egeon, Gaoler, Officers, and other Attendants)

(Meanwhile in the town of Ephesus, enter Antipholus of Syracuse, First Merchant and Dromio of Syracuse)

FIRST MERCHANT: So, what brings you here to Ephesus? Business? The majority of Epidamium visitors come to Ephesus for business.

ANTIPHOLUS OF SYRACUSE: Yes, we'd heard Ephesus is a good place for business, and since Epidamium is so close, we figured we'd go check it out.

FIRST MERCHANT: Well then, I hope you have a good stay in our small town. I am sure you will have a pleasant time with our people. You can stay in the nearby motel. And you know my address; drop by whenever you need something.

ANTIPHOLUS OF SYRACUSE: Thank you, my friend. I will be eternally grateful for your generosity to us two strangers.

(Exeunt)

SCENE 2

(In Ephesus, Antipholus of Syracuse and Dromio of Syracuse enter the market)

ANTIPHOLUS OF SYRACUSE: Nobody should know that we are from Syracuse and not from Epidamium. If anybody finds out, our plan will fail and we will never be able to find our brothers.

DROMIO OF SYRACUSE: But how are we going to find them? The town might be small but a place is never too small to find a person you know nothing about. And we cannot get caught. It will be more difficult since we look alike. People will confuse us for our twins.

ANTIPHOLUS OF SYRACUSE: We have to be clever and discrete. We cannot afford to be discovered. We both understand how important it is for us to find them. Finding them is the only way to reunite our family, and mother may also return. *(Handing money to Dromio)* Here, take this money and go find us a place to stay. And remember, if anyone asks, we are from Epidamium.

(Exits Dromio of Syracuse)

(To himself) I really hope we find our brothers.

(Enter Dromio of Ephesus)

DROMIO OF EPHESUS: What are you doing here? Supper is ready, let's go home.

ANTIPHOLUS OF SYRACUSE: What is this Dromio? Where is the money that I gave you? Did you find us a place to stay?

DROMIO OF EPHESUS: What place? Anyways did you hear? They caught a man from Syracuse. But he was excused for some reason. There are plenty of rumours going around the town.

ANTIPHOLUS OF SYRACUSE: Shhhh! Nobody should know that we are from Syracuse. I told you;

Be discrete and clever. We have to find our twins and get back home to unite our family. Now go and book the room.

DROMIO OF EPHESUS:*(Shocked as realisation hits)* Yes! A place to stay! I will go right away.

(Exits Dromio of Ephesus)

ANTIPHOLUS OF SYRACUSE: What's the matter with this guy? This time, he'd better do what I told him to do.

(Dromio of Syracuse enters)

DROMIO OF SYRACUSE: I found a place to stay master. We can go and rest now.

(Antipholus and Dromio of Syracuse exits. Enter Antipholus of Ephesus running behind Dromio of Ephesus)

ANTIPHOLUS OF EPHESUS: Are you sure it was him?

DROMIO OF EPHESUS: Yes, he even said he is from Syracuse and that they are here to find us and take us back home. Our wish has finally come true. They have finally come to take us home. We should go and tell them that it's us and we can go back now.

ANTIPHOLUS OF EPHESUS: So, they have finally come. But why now? Why after so many years?

DROMIO OF EPHESUS: That is no longer relevant. All that matters is that they have arrived to transport us home. Let's go!

ANTIPHOLUS OF SYRACUSE: No! We are not going back with them.

DROMIO OF EPHESUS: What are you saying? Why will we not go with them? We waited so many years after the shipwreck and now that they have finally come.

ANTIPHOLUS OF EPHESUS: We are not going with them. We are going as them. Think about it; they could have come long back to get us. If they knew that we were here, why did they take this many years to come? They didn't need us all this time, and now that they do, they believe they can get us back? NO! We will return. But not with them. We'll kill them and then return as them.

DROMIO OF EPHESUS: Are you serious? You want to murder them? They are our brothers. How can we do this to them?

ANTIPHOLUS OF EPHESUS: The same way they left us alone and did not return for a long time. It is now time for vengeance. We must now follow them around. If we want to adopt their identity, we must learn to act, speak, and behave like them.

DROMIO OF EPHESUS: Are you certain about it? Consider it again.

ANTIPHOLUS OF EPHESUS: Yes! There's no going back now. We will follow them wherever they go. We have to be successful in this if we want to go back.

(Exeunt)

SCENE 3

(Enter Antipholus of Syracuse and Dromio of Syracuse)

DROMIO OF SYRACUSE: It has been a week and there is no clue of them. I don't think they are here. What do you say? Should we go back?

ANTIPHOLUS OF SYRACUSE: We cannot give up so early. Let's look for them for a few more days and see. I have a feeling that they are here. I feel it in my heart.

DROMIO OF SYRACUSE: If that's what you say then fine. Let's go into the alleys instead of the market, we might find a sign of them.

(Exit Antipholus of Syracuse and Dromio of Syracuse)

(Enter Antipholus of Ephesus and Dromio of Ephesus)

ANTIPHOLUS OF SYRACUSE: Focus! Keep an eye on them. Take note of everything they do and emulate it from now on. Examine your twin's gait. Even that should be copied.

DROMIO OF EPHESUS: What if we get caught? Yesterday I was this close to getting caught by my twin. I think this is a bad idea. We should just go with them.

ANTIPHOLUS OF SYRACUSE: Are you crazy? We have to go forward with the plan. I almost got caught yesterday, you'll have to be more cautious from now on. Now follow my instructions.

(Exit Antipholus of Ephesus and Dromio of Ephesus)

(Enter Egeon and Second Merchant)

SECOND MERCHANT: I am sure it was them. The way you described them, I saw them in the market a few days ago. They claim to be here to do business from Epidamium.

EGEON: Epidamium you say? It has to be them. I am sure I will find my son in no time.

(Exeunt)

SCENE 4

(Enter Dromio of Ephesus)

DROMIO OF EPHESUS: This is a disaster. Master has gone insane. Why would he wish to murder them? If he wasn't so angry at them, we could all go back home safe and happy. But the thought of vengeance has blinded the master. He is so desperate for vengeance that he is willing to murder his own twin. In the process, I will lose my twin. Loyalty is putting me to the test right now. I'm being pulled in two directions: by loyalty and by blood.

(Enter Dromio of Syracuse)

DROMIO OF SYRACUSE: Am I dreaming? Is it really you?

Oh! How long I have waited for this day to come. I finally meet you, my brother, my twin. You do not know how much I have longed to see you.

DROMIO OF EPHESUS:(*shocked*) It's you. You have finally come to get me. I have always wished for this day to come brother.

DROMIO OF SYRACUSE: (Hugging his brother) Oh how happy I am! Master will be so delighted to know that I have finally found you. Let's go to him.

DROMIO OF EPHESUS: No, we should each go to our respective masters and inform them of this wonderful news. And let's meet with our masters again tomorrow at our house.

DROMIO OF SYRACUSE: Yes, let's do that. I will go and tell master now. We will meet tomorrow and go back home together.

(Exit Dromio of Syracuse)

(Enter Antipholus of Ephesus)

ANTIPHOLUS OF EPHESUS: Dromio, you did an excellent job. Our wish will be granted tomorrow.

(Exeunt)

SCENE 5

(Enter Antipholus of Ephesus, Dromio of Ephesus, Antipholus of Syracuse and Dromio of Syracuse in Antipholus of Ephesus's house.)

ANTIPHOLUS OF EPHESUS: I hope you like my humble house.

ANTIPHOLUS OF SYRACUSE: It's lovely! Oh brother! How delighted I finally get to meet you after all these years. I am so happy that we can finally all go back home and hopefully mother also comes back.

ANTIPHOLUS OF EPHESUS: Oh, she certainly will. Now that both her sons will be back, she will come back in no time. Have some tea my brother. Dromio.

ANTIPHOLUS OF SYRACUSE: How happy you must be Dromio to meet your brother. You waited so many years dreaming about this day.

DROMIO OF EPHESUS: I am certainly overjoyed. What a lovely moment.

(The pairs of twins go in for a hug. Both the pairs of Ephesus stab their twin)

ANTIPHOLUS OF SYRACUSE: What have you done my brother?

ANTIPHOLUS OF EPHESUS: What were your thoughts? Will you return after all these years, and we will forgive you? Do you realise how much we've suffered in this town for so long, surrounded by strangers? We had no idea what was in store for us in the future. You have no idea how long we have struggled. We will return, but without you, as you are. Do you feel the pain that we felt all these years?

(To Dromio of Ephesus)

Go get rid of their bodies. Bury them behind the empty park where no one will find them. And get ready to go back home. Remember that you are Dromio of Syracuse from tomorrow.

(Dromio obeys his master with tears in his eyes while grieving his brother's death)

(Next day, Enter Egeon running upon seeing Antipholus and Dromio waiting in line to get on the ship back to Ephesus)

EGEON: My son! Why did you leave like that? You know how dangerous it is for you to be here. Let's go back home now.

ANTIPHOLUS Of EPHESUS: (Pretending to be Antipholus of Syracuse) Yes father. I sincerely apologise for leaving in such a hasty manner. I'm ready to go home right now.

EGEON:(*Suspicious*) We must first visit Duke Solinus. To tell him about you. Come with me, both of you, and we'll start our journey back home later that evening.

(Exeunt)

XXII
REALMS OF HARMONY - ESTHER RANI

SCENE 1

(In the opulent royal court of Eldoria. King Leofric is seated on his throne, attended by a group of nobles. Princess Seraphina stands beside her father, King Leofric, with an air of reluctance)

KING LEOFRIC: (Addressing the nobles)My loyal subjects, the time has come to address matters of utmost importance. As you know, our realm thrives through alliances and unity.

(The nobles nod in agreement)

KING LEOFRIC: (Continuing) Today, I announce the betrothal of my beloved daughter, Princess Seraphina, to Prince Corwin of the distant realm of Veridia. This union will strengthen our kingdom and ensure our prosperity.

(There is polite applause from the nobles, but Seraphina's expression shows her reluctance)

PRINCESS SERAPHINA: (Whispers to herself) Another strategic alliance...

(Lady Thalassa, a cunning courtier, approaches Seraphina with a sly smile)

LADY THALASSA: (Whispers to Seraphina) A wise decision, Your Highness, securing the future of Eldoria.

(Seraphina forces a smile in response)

KING LEOFRIC: (Addressing the court) Let the preparations for the engagement ceremony begin. We shall celebrate this alliance in grand fashion.

(The nobles continue to offer polite applause)

(As the court disperses, Seraphina's gaze lingers on a distant tapestry depicting two lovers, hinting at her unspoken desires)

(In Princess Seraphina's lavishly decorated chambers. She is alone, gazing out of a window at the moonlit garden. A sense of melancholy surrounds her.)

PRINCESS SERAPHINA: (Sighs deeply) Another night... and the weight of duty presses upon me.

(Seraphina's loyal maid, Lyria, enters the room quietly. She observes Seraphina's pensive mood)

LYRIA: (Softly) Your Highness, your thoughts seem heavy tonight.

PRINCESS SERAPHINA: (Turns to Lyria with a wistful smile) Oh, Lyria, how I long for a life of my own choosing, one where love isn't sacrificed for the kingdom's sake.

(Lyria approaches Seraphina and offers a comforting embrace.)

LYRIA: (Whispers soothingly)Your heart is your own, Princess, and no betrothal can change that.

PRINCESS SERAPHINA: (Nods, her resolve strengthening) You're right, Lyria. I mustn't forget who I am. I won't let this arranged marriage define me.

(Lyria smiles, understanding the determination in Seraphina's eyes.)

LYRIA: (Encouragingly) You're strong, Your Highness, and love has a way of finding its path, even though the darkest of forests.

(Seraphina's gaze returns to the moonlit garden)

PRINCESS SERAPHINA: (Softly) Perhaps, in the hidden corners of this kingdom, there's a love waiting to be discovered, a love that will echo through the ages.

(Seraphina's internal conflict and foreshadows her determination to seek love and authenticity in her life, even in the face of societal expectations)

SCENE 2

(In a moonlit garden within the palace grounds. Seraphina, wearing a cloak, waits anxiously by the garden's fountain. Aldric, disguised as a commoner, enters cautiously)

PRINCESS SERAPHINA: (Whispers with relief) Aldric, you came.

ALDRIC: (Approaching Seraphina) How could I resist, my love?

(They embrace, their love evident)

PRINCESS SERAPHINA: (Pulls away, worried) We must be cautious, Aldric. Our love is our greatest secret.

ALDRIC: (Nods) I understand. But our love is worth any risk.

(Their hands touch, and they share a passionate kiss)

LADY THALASSA: (Emerges from the shadows, sinister) How sweet young love can be.

(Seraphina and Aldric break apart in shock.)

PRINCESS SERAPHINA:(Angry and defiant) Lady Thalassa! You've been spying on us!

LADY THALASSA:(Smirking)I couldn't resist a midnight stroll in the garden, Your Highness.

ALDRIC:(Steps forward, protective) Stay away from Princess Seraphina.

LADY THALASSA: (Taunting) Oh, how gallant. But your love will be your undoing.

(Lady Thalassa leaves, leaving Seraphina and Aldric shaken.)

PRINCESS SERAPHINA: (Resolute) We can't let her control our destiny, Aldric.

ALDRIC: (Holding Seraphina's hand) I'll find a way for us to be together, no matter the obstacles.

(They share a final, longing look before parting)

(In Lady Thalassa's opulent chamber within the palace. She stands near a window, her expression sly)

LADY THALASSA:(Talking to herself, plotting)A secret love, a forbidden affair - the perfect weapon.

(As Lady Thalassa contemplates her next move, a knock at the door interrupts her thoughts. She composes herself quickly.)

KING LEOFRIC: (Entering) Lady Thalassa, I seek your counsel on the upcoming engagement.

LADY THALASSA: (Curtsies) Of course, Your Majesty. Your daughter's happiness is my utmost concern.

KING LEOFRIC:(*Serious*) It has come to my attention that Princess Seraphina may have feelings for someone else. Is this true?

(Lady Thalassa feigns surprise)

LADY THALASSA:(*Innocently*) Your Majesty, I have heard nothing of the sort.

KING LEOFRIC:(*Doubtful*) Lady Thalassa, I sense there is more to this than meets the eye. If you learn anything, inform me immediately.

(King Leofric exits, leaving Lady Thalassa with a devious smile.)

LADY THALASSA: (Whispers to herself) The King's trust is my key to power. And power, dear Seraphina, is what I seek.

(Lady Thalassa determined to exploit the knowledge of Seraphina's secret love for her own gain)

SCENE 3

(In Aldric's modest workshop, filled with various artisan tools and crafts. Aldric is alone, deep in thought)

ALDRIC: (Muttering to himself) There must be a way, a path to unite our love.

(Aldric paces around the room, his determination growing. He notices a weathered map on the wall, depicting ancient paths through the kingdom)

ALDRIC: (Eureka moment) The Unity Seekers! The old stories speak of their wisdom.

(He retrieves a hidden journal and starts sketching a plan)

(Transitions to the palace garden, where Seraphina, Lyria, and Aldric meet under the moonlight. Aldric presents the journal to Seraphina)

PRINCESS SERAPHINA:*(Curious)* What is this, Aldric?

ALDRIC: *(Excited)* It's a map, a guide to the Unity Seekers' hidden world. They may hold the key to uniting our love and revealing hidden truths.

LYRIA:*(Supportive)* It's a daring plan, but we have no choice.

(They share a determined look, united in their quest)

(Back to the palace court, where King Leofric addresses the nobles)

KING LEOFRIC: *(Resolute)* My dear subjects, the time has come to embrace change and unity. Princess Seraphina has shown me the path to a brighter future.

(Aldric, Seraphina, and Lyria enter the court, followed by scholars and Unity Seekers)

ALDRIC:*(Addressing the court)* We seek unity, understanding, and the power of true love to guide our kingdom.

PRINCESS SERAPHINA:(With conviction, looking at Aldric) I choose love over duty, for love is the harmony that shall bind our realms.

(The court erupts in applause and agreement)

XXIII
THE ROYAL STAUNCH - ADITYA PRINCE GEORGE

SCENE 1

(Inside the Majestic Court of Kingdom of Madeira)

(Enter King Ferdinand and Princess Georgina)

KING FERDINAND: My dear Georgina, it is time for you to consider marriage.

PRINCESS GEORGINA: I understand father.

KING FERDINAND: Isn't it true that you've grown so quickly, my dear?

PRINCESS GEORGINA: You're always saying that...

KING FERDINAND: Right, my dear child, I can't believe how quickly time passes.

PRINCESS GEORGINA: That is how life is, father.

(Princess Georgina leaning onto her dad)

KING FERDINAND: My dear child, I have something to say.

PRINCESS GEORGINA: Go on dad, is it about marriage.

KING FERDINAND: Yes, my child, you read me like your mother. Lionel, a nobleman from our province, is interested in you.

PRINCESS GEORGINA: Father, I appreciate your concern. But I long to marry for love, not political alliances.

KING FERDINAND: You are free to think about it at your leisure, my dear. I have to attend to my work now.

PRINCESS GEORGINA: Okay dad, see you.

(King Ferdinand left the Court)

(Exeunt)

SCENE 2

(A humble Servant's quarters in the Madeira Castle)

(Prince Cristiano disguised as newly appointed gardener named Zlatan, enters the room)

SERVANT ALEXIA: Who is this?

PRINCE CRISTIANO: Don't panic my brothers and sisters, I am Prince Cristiano from the neighbouring kingdom of Lisbon, and I am captivated by the beauty of Georgina. HECTOR knows me.

(Servants surprised)

SERVANT HECTOR: My Lord, I couldn't spot you dressed in bright apparel. Prince Alexander, allow me to acquaint you with the servants who work tirelessly to maintain the palace. This is Alexia, our head maid, and Thomas, the head butler.

PRINCE CRISTIANO: Pleasure to meet you both. I appreciate the effort you put into ensuring the smooth operation of the palace.

SERVANT ALEXIA: Thank you, Your Highness. We take great pride in our work, and it's always a pleasure to have a visit from a member of the royal family.

SERVANT THOMAS: Indeed, Your Highness. We strive to provide the best service and support for the king and his esteemed guests.

PRINCE CRISTIANO: I admire your dedication and attention to detail. The palace truly reflects the hard work of its staff. I am grateful for all that you do.

SERVANT HECTOR: I still cannot believe you managed to get here disguised.

PRINCE CRISTIANO (DISGUISED AS ZLATAN): Ah, if only Georgina could see beyond my disguise.

SERVANT ALEXIA: Prince Cristiano, if there is anything we can do to make your visit more comfortable, please do not hesitate to let us know. We are always at your service.

PRINCE CRISTIANO: That is very kind of you. I appreciate your offer, and I'm sure I will enjoy my time here at the palace.

(Exeunt)

SCENE 3

(Princess Georgina and Prince Cristiano disguised as Zlatan the Gardner talking in the garden behind the castle)

PRINCESS GEORGINA: Zlatan, there is something about you that draws me in. Your kindness and wit have captured my heart. Tell me, who are you really?

PRINCE CRISTIANO: Yes, my lady, I am Prince Cristiano from the neighbouring kingdom of Lisbon. I had to disguise myself as a gardener to get close to you, for I feared that my true identity would complicate things. But know that every word I've spoken and every moment we've shared has been genuine.

PRINCE GEORGINA: Prince Cristiano? This is unexpected! I had no idea of your royal status. But it doesn't matter to me because I'm falling in love with you, not your title or wealth.

PRINCE CRISTIANO: Your words fill me with joy, Georgina. My intent was always to win your heart honestly, not through deceit. I am relieved that you see beyond the disguise and appreciate the true character within me.

PRINCESS GEORGINA: Let us put aside any pretences or barriers that may exist between us, Cristiano. I've grown to care deeply for you, and I believe our connection was meant to be. How can we make our love known to the rest of the world?

PRINCE CRISTIANO: My lady, I adore you and I wish for nothing more than to proclaim our love openly. However, we must approach this with caution. Lionel still seeks your hand in marriage, and if he discovers our feelings, he may use it to his advantage.

PRINCESS GEORGINA: You are right, Cristiano. We must exercise caution and devise a strategy to protect our love from Lionel's schemes. But I believe that if we work together, we can overcome any obstacle and protect what is true and pure between us.

PRINCE CRISTIANO: Your courage inspires me, Georgina. I promise to stand by your side, to defend our love, and to find a way for us to be together, despite the obstacles we may face.

PRINCESS GEORGINA: And I promise to be patient and believe in our bond, knowing that true love can overcome any obstacle. Cristiano, let our hearts guide us, and may our love grow stronger with each passing day.

(Exeunt)

SCENE 4

(Lionel plotting in his room)

(Neymaro entered his room)

Lionel: It infuriates me that Georgina is drawn to this Cristiano fellow. I must find a way to tarnish his reputation.

NEYMARO: My lord, I have an idea. We could spread rumours about his true identity, hoping to make it difficult between him and the princess.

LIONEL: Yeah, that's it. Capturing Georgina will force him to come to our hideout.

NEYMARO: Yes, my Lord, I will divert the king's attention by engaging him in some activity.

(Exeunt)

SCENE 5

(Cristiano comes looking for Georgina in Lionel's hideout)

CRISTIANO: Georgina, where are you? I will not rest until I find you and keep you safe from Lionel.

(Suddenly Lionel pops in with Georgina in her custody)

LIONEL: Georgina! I've captured her! She will be mine, whether you like it or not.

CRISTIANO: Lionel, release Georgina at once! I will not let your selfish desires stand in the way of true love.

(Lionel pulls out the sword and kept it on her neck)

LIONEL: If you don't leave this place right now, this sword shall slash her throat.

(Georgina pushed and moves away from Lionel, Cristiano pulls out his sword and the duel between Cristiano and Lionel begun)

CRISTIANO: There is no way you are going to take her while I am alive.

(Cristiano's confrontations threw Lionel off balance and brought him under his control)

LIONEL: Leave me alone or she will be killed by my people.

(Trying to breathe from his deadlock)

CRISTIANO: Well, you won't be there to tell them.

(Cristiano defeats Lionel and rescues Georgina)

(Exeunt)

SCENE 6

(Cristiano returning to the Castle of Madeira with Georgina)

KING FERDINAND: My gratitude, Zlatan, knows no bounds. You have rescued my daughter and my kingdom from a treacherous traitor. I give you my blessing, and I may reward you. Tell me what you desire.

(Cristiano removes the disguise and reveals himself as the Prince of Lisbon)

KING FERDINAND: Prince Cristiano, you?

CRISTIANO: Yes, my Lord, her beauty captivated me and compelled me to do all of this.

KING FERDINAND: Do you fancy the princess?

CRISTIANO: Yes, my Lord, I fell to her profound beauty and not to her title.

KING FERDINAND: Princess, how do you feel about him?

(Georgina holds Cristiano's hands)

GEORGINA: We have overcome such adversity together, Cristiano. Above all, I prefer you. Allow our love to lead us into a bright future.

KING FERDINAND: Let the feasting begin!!

(The kingdom is rejoiced as Cristiano and Georgina celebrate their love)

(Exeunt)

XXIV
UNVEILING GREED AND BETRAYAL - PRIYANKA E

SCENE 1

(Enter Timon and Dexter)

DEXTER: Good morning, Timon.

TIMON: I am delighted to find you in good health.

DEXTER: It has been very long since our paths crossed.

TIMON: The world is expanding as it grows. Pray for a fairer world.

DEXTER: Yes, that is a commonly expressed truth in recent times.

TIMON: My wealth is very important to me, and it will be guarded with the vigilance of a sentinel, because I will not let knaves and villains touch it.

DEXTER: That is perfectly said by Timon. But beware, for wealth like the serpent's tongue can entice with its gleaming scales.

TOMON: Dexter, your words ring like the church bells on a Sunday morning. I share your sentiments.

(Exists Timon and Dexter)

SCENE 2

(Enter Paulina and Lizzie)

LIZZIE: Do you know where Timon has hidden the suitcase keys, Paulina?

PAULINA: (laughs) I do.

LIZZIE: That is excellent news.

PAULINA: I shall examine the treasures then.

LIZZIE: Have you informed Doricles?

PAULINA: He is making his here and he shall arrive soon.

LIZZIE: well.

(Lizzie exits)

(Enter Doricles)

DORICLES: Are all preparations completed?

PAULINA: Yes, they are.

DORICLES: Good, then let us proceed.

PAULINA: Very well, my love.

(They both set forth on their journey, departing the village, taking with them all its riches.)

(Enter Saunders, Falconer and Lucullus)

SAUNDERS: Stop there! Do they not resemble Paulina?

LAUCULLUS: Aye. Yeah

DEXTER: Let us apprehend them before they flee!

SAUNDERS: Have you both sought to plunder Timon's riches?

PAULINA: (Laughs) Yes.

SAUNDERS: Aren't you ashamed of such deeds?

PAULINA: No, God, he has plenty. Taking a fraction is not a sin.

SAUNDERS: I must immediately notify Timon of this.

DEXTER: I shall bring Timon here.

FALCONER: Make haste!

(Enter Timon)

TIMON: Please, someone enlighten me on this uproar.

SAUNDERS: Timon, your wife was on the verge of fleeing with your fortune.

TIMON: What! Such treachery had never occurred to me.

DEXTER: Why would you do such an act?

PAULINA: I am not obliged to render an explanation to this!

SAUNDERS: Timon should stop conversing with this pair. Allow us to transport them to the king's court.

FALCONER: That is a prudent course, indeed.

(Paulina and Doricles are both imprisoned.)

SCENE 3

LIZZIE: Timon please, don't worry. (*She consoles him*)

TIMON: I'm afraid I can't. My mind is a tormented prison, and my eyes are filled with tears.

LIZZIE: Timon, take my advice. Not all beautiful flowers have the same sweet fragrance.

TIMON: My wits have run out, and mine heart bears wounds deep as the ocean's abyss.

LIZZIE: (soothingly) Henceforth, you must learn where to avoid dangerous paths.

TIMON: (in reluctant agreement) I must accept my predicament.

LIZZIE: Timon, I would like to reveal a secret to you!

TIMON: Speak on, Lizzie.

LIZZIE: I know where Paulina has concealed the—-

TIMON: Tell me, where is it hidden?

LIZZIE: Come hither with me, and I shall reveal it to you.

(Both Lizzie and Timon proceed to the place where the wealth had been concealed.)

(Lizzie and Timon goes to the cave)

LIZZIE: This is the place, Timon, behold!

TIMON: Did Paulina hide it away in this very spot?

LIZZIE: Yeah, could you please wait for me until I return in a few minutes?

TIMON: Yes, be careful.

(Lizzie returns and stabs him with a knife. He falls to the ground, bleeding)

TIMON: Lizzie, how could you...? I had trust in you.

LIZZIE: I too, had trusted you Timon. But times have changed. Rest in peace, my love.

(Timon breathes his last...breath)

SCENE 4

(Paulina and Doricles had been released from prison)

PAULINA: I never imagined my life would be so miserable. I could have lived content with the dreams I once held dear, but those times are long gone.

DORICLES: What's the matter with you? Stop your endless lamentations. I'm irritated and annoyed.

PAULINA: It is the torment I bear within myself every day. How can you possibly be so heartless?

DORICLES: So, you think I'm devoid of emotion? As if to assert, I am unconcerned. Did I act solely for my own enjoyment and satisfaction?

PAULINA: Very well then, let me be as self-serving as you.

DORICLES: I'm leaving for my work. We'll meet again this evening.

(At evening, she waits for her husband)

PAULINA: Where has he vanished? It is getting late. He should have returned by now. My heart is heavy with anxiety.

(She waits near the doorsteps)

SCENE 5

(Enter Saunders and Doricles at Lizzie's house)

SAUNDERS: Lizzie, please open the doors! Why are they kept shut? Doricles, please wait while she unlatches the door.

(He encounters Paulina in front of the door)

DORICLES: Paulina? What brings you out here?

PAULINA: Doricles, what are you doing in this place?

(Lizzie arrives and observes them)

LIZZIE: My apologies. We can't provide you with anything hereafter. Depart, from here you commoner. (She turns to Doricles)Doricles, do you know this woman?

DORICLES: No, I have no knowledge of this commoner! Lizzie slams the door, leaving Paulina outside

PAULINA: I believe the Almighty is punishing me because my sins are numerous! Trust is a luxury I will never have! I should have been content with the life Timon had bestowed upon me. Now I am alone with no one. Greed has consumed me, and I am destitute.

(Paulina proceeds to the place where Timon met his end and takes her own life)

(Exeunt)

XXV
HEARTS IN QUARANTINE - ALEENA SHAJAN

ACT 1: *The cure within*

(The play is set when the quarantine period had begun due to the spread of Covid-19. VedicPharm and DeltaMedix Pharmaceuticals are competing to establish a strong reputation by discovering a cure for Covid 19The stage is split into two. On one side we have a dimly lit messy room. A computer table is kept in one corner and a wardrobe with laboratory equipment in the other. Aarav is seated in front of the computer, his back hunched, wearing headphones. The screen casts a glow on his face. On the other side, we have the cozy-looking bedroom of Nira, with a vintage wooden nightstand holding a delicate lamp, casting a warm glow on her face. On the adjacent wall, a bookshelf overflows with fairy tales, young adult novels, and journals. Nira is deep in thought with a pen and a thick book on her lap)

SCENE 1

(The spotlight on Aarav)

NARRATOR: Adithya Sharma, the CEO of VedicPharm, is Aarav's father. He is a scientist with a mind as fast as his lab's centrifuge. He is currently working hard to find a cure for the COVID-19 virus which is killing many innocent people and leaving many in pain and agony. He has already finished his research and drafted the first vaccine formula. However, there are still steps to take in order to put the formula into action. But now, tired from his long day, Aarav is looking for a distraction to simply relax. He's going through some virtual events and listening to poems written by different people.

(The spotlight dims, and now the focus is on Nira)

NARRATOR: This is Nira Shetty, the only granddaughter of Nakul Shetty, the chairman and managing director of DeltaMedix Pharmaceuticals. She lost her parents when she was seven, and her grandparents have been caring for her ever since. She is never left alone and is always surrounded and supported by her relatives and cousins. She is a highly motivated individual. She refuses to run the family business or settle down in life. She would rather be a poet. She wants to live life and enjoy literature. Although she is extremely gifted, she has never had the opportunity to exhibit it. She is now excited to present her poem in a virtual poetry event.

(Lights dim)

(The virtual poetry session has begun. It is Nira's turn to recite her poem. She is very excited and nervous. She begins to recite her verses.)

NIRA: In a world of hues and shades so wide,

Stands a lover with honey brown eyes.

A blend of golden sun and earth's embrace,

A glimpse of nature's tender grace.

With every regard, they feel to say,

Stories of warmth and sunlit days.

Eyes that glimmer, a caramel dream,

Soft as dusk and morning's beam.

In those depths, one could easily dive,

A universe where dreams come alive.

Mysteries unfold, secrets are told,

By honey brown eyes, both youthful and old.

Gentle and wild, calm yet profound,

Similar is the appeal, in those eyes I have found.

For in that gaze, love's promise lies,

Forever held in honey brown eyes.

(She looks up at the screen and is amazed to see the tons of emojis appearing on her screen. The audience loved it. Notification sounds of emoji's pop up)

AARAV:(Muttering to himself) How can someone be so beautiful? She is just heavenly, and her words, captivating. Her words flow like a gentle river, bringing life to everything in their path.

(The reading ends and a talk box pops up for the attendees. They can talk to their favourite reciters on a video chat. Aarav immediately clicks on it. After a few minutes of waiting, they were here, together on a call, with nobody else. Aarav's happiness knew no bounds)

NIRA: Good evening, Aarav. So, did you enjoy my poetry? I'd love to hear your thoughts so I can improve for my next recitation.

AARAV: This is the first time I've been interested in such things, and I must say you did not disappoint. It was fantastic. To be honest, I was just looking for something to do. And, I must say, I came across the best one. If all poets are as enthralling as you, I might become a regular. Your words... they made an impression.

NIRA:(with a playful smirk) Ah, so fate brought you to my poetry night. I hope it was a pleasant distraction.

AARAV: (Chuckling) Oh, it was. And it's not just the poetry; it's the poet too. Those hazel eyes are quite captivating.

NIRA: Well, aren't you a smooth talker? I should probably warn you that compliments may cause me to recite more poems.

AARAV: In that case, let me shower you with some more. How about a virtual coffee sometime? We can share poems, stories, or just gaze at each other through webcams.

NIRA: Gazing into webcams? Now, that's a 21st-century romance. I'd be up for that. As long as you promise to share some of your own poems as well.

AARAV: Deal! But, fair warning, I might just write one about a mesmerising poet with hazel eyes.

NIRA: The tables have been turned! Now I'm the one looking for a distraction. Mr. Aarav, I'm looking forward to our virtual date. But let me move on; I have a few more people on the list. I'll talk to you later. Bye.

AARAV: Oh, okay. Thank you for your time. See you.

(The chat ends, and Aarav finds himself smiling. The evening has taken an unexpected turn for him, and he couldn't be happier about it. Both log out with the intention of reconnecting, and as the screen fades, the spark of a new connection remains)

SCENE 2

(Aarav and Nira are having a video call. Nira is sitting next to her bookshelf. A family photograph is kept in the background. Aarav is seated, as usual, with his headphones on)

AARAV: (looking at a picture behind Nira) Is that your family? I think I recognize some faces.

NIRA: Oh, yes, that's from our annual company gala. My parents, my siblings, and me.

AARAV: (squinting) Wait a minute, isn't that the logo for Delta Medix Pharmaceuticals?

NIRA: Yes, my family owns it. Why?

AARAV: (taking a deep breath) Nira, my family runs Vedic Pharm. We've been competitors with Delta Medix Pharmaceuticals for decades.

NIRA: (eyes widening) Oh my God... Vedic Pharm? As in the biggest rival to our company? This is... unexpected.

AARAV: To say the least. No wonder our families had "differences" we spoke of earlier.

NIRA: I never connected the dots. I knew about the business rivalry, of course, but never thought I'd be talking to Vedic Pharm heir.

AARAV: Neither did I. But Nira, we're not our families. We're not our companies.

NIRA: True, but it complicates things, doesn't it?

AARAV: Only if we let it. Our connection, our conversations, they're all ours. Not tied to business or legacy.

NIRA: (sighing) I hope it can remain that way. Can we keep this... us... away from all the corporate politics?

AARAV: I want nothing more.

NIRA: Let's get through this together. After all, who would've thought such rivals would bond over poetry?

AARAV: (smiling) Life has its own poetry, doesn't it? (Adjusting his camera, lab equipment in the background)

NIRA: (smiling, a canopy of fairy lights above her) Likewise, Aarav. Your lab looks intense! Always a scientist, huh?

AARAV: Always. Just as you're always surrounded by your cosy lights and books. By the way, I enjoyed your poetry the other night.

NIRA: Thank you. You know, it's one of my dreams to publish my own poetry book someday. To make sure my words bridge gaps, especially those that seem insurmountable...like the one between our families.

AARAV: (sighing)Ah, the infamous family feud. You know, it's ironic. Here we are, connected by verses and video calls, yet separated by a legacy we didn't choose.

NIRA:(coughing) Isn't that the story of life? Inherited dreams, inherited conflicts. But hey, we're redefining that narrative, aren't we?

AARAV: Absolutely. We are more than the stories passed down to us.

(There's a moment of silence, broken by Nira's cough)

AARAV: (concern evident in his eyes)Nira, are you okay? You've been coughing.

NIRA: It's just the changing weather. Don't worry. I'm fine.

AARAV: Are you sure?

NIRA: Yes. So, about our next virtual date... How about a movie night?

AARAV: Sounds perfect. How about next Friday?

NIRA: It's a date!

(Next Friday, Aarav waits. Nira doesn't log on.)

AARAV: (voice message) Nira, is everything okay? We had our movie night planned.

(Nira calls him the next afternoon)

NIRA:(after a long pause) Aarav, I'm so sorry. I've been tested positive for COVID-19. I didn't want to stress you out.

AARAV:(*shocked*) Oh, Nira... Why didn't you tell me earlier? How are you feeling?

NIRA: I thought it was just a cold... I didn't expect this.

AARAV: Please, promise me you'll take care of yourself.

NIRA: I promise, I'll get through this. We still have a lot of virtual dates ahead.

AARAV: Yes, we do. And when you're better, maybe... maybe we can even meet in person. Dreams are worth fighting for, remember?

NIRA: (smiling weakly)I'll remember. I need to rest now.

AARAV: Rest up. Get well soon. I'll be looking forward to our next date.

NIRA: Thanks, Aarav. Goodnight.

AARAV: Goodnight, Nira.

(They both log out. Nira falls asleep. Aarav appears concerned and rushes to his lab to conduct an experiment)

(Lights dim. Exeunt)

SCENE 3

(Nira and Aarav are on a video call. Nira is dozing off on the bed. On a nearby table, some tablets are kept. Aarav is in the lab, surrounded by test tubes and chemicals. Little scraps of paper were scattered about)

AARAV: Nira? Can you hear me?

NIRA: Yes, Aarav. The connection, like me, is frail.

AARAV: What matters is that you're still fighting. Now, tell me about the symptoms in detail.

NIRA: Okay. So, it started with what I thought was simply exhaustion. Then the headaches became constant, like a vice grip on my temples.

AARAV: And these headaches, do they worsen at any particular time of day?

NIRA: They're most intense in the evening. There is more. I'm constantly out of breath, as if I've just ran a marathon.

AARAV: Shortness of breath. Noted. Are there specific activities that trigger it more?

NIRA: Simple things, Aarav. Even just walking to the kitchen.

AARAV: Alright, keep going.

NIRA: Everything tastes... metallic. And drinking water feels impossible.

AARAV: Change in taste and difficulty swallowing. Do you experience any sharp shooting pains?

NIRA: Yes, right in the chest. And some nights, the pain radiates to my back.

AARAV: Nira, any temperature changes? Feeling too hot or too cold?

NIRA: (*sighing deeply*) It's erratic. Sometimes, I'm shivering; at other times, I feel like I'm on fire. Oh, and the throat... feels like I have sandpaper in there!

AARAV: Temperature fluctuations and throat pain... Tell me, any sensory changes? Vision, hearing?

NIRA: Vision's fine. But there's this maddening ringing in my ears. It's like a never-ending echo.

AARAV: Anything else you've observed? No matter how minor it seems.

NIRA Bluish fingertips. They terrify me, Aarav. What does that mean?

AARAV: Could be circulation. But we'll get to the bottom of this. Continue.

NIRA: Some nights, my sheets are drenched in sweat. And emotionally, it's a roller coaster. Moments of intense fear followed by numbness.

AARAV: Okay. Mood swings, night sweats. I'm piecing this together. You said about despair earlier?

NIRA: Yes. It's this heavy cloud that won't lift. Some days are tougher than the others.

AARAV: *(worried)* Your mental well-being is important too. I'm noting everything down. Have you experienced any joint pain or muscle stiffness?

NIRA: My joints, especially the knees, ache. And my muscles feel like I've been lifting weights.

AARAV: Joint pain, muscle stiffness... Nira, I'm mapping all this out. It's giving me some direction.

NIRA: *(coughing)* Sorry, the coughing is getting worse.

AARAV: Nira, try to calm down. Slow breaths.

NIRA: I'm trying, Aarav. It's just so hard.

AARAV: Nira? Nira, stay with me!

NIRA: I'm here. But I should rest soon.

AARAV: And I promise you that I will do everything in my power to assist you.

NIRA: I believe in you, Aarav.

AARAV: Thank you, Nira. Rest well. I won't give up.

NIRA: (weakly) Me too, Aarav. Neither on me nor you.

(The screen goes dark, leaving Aarav amidst scattered papers, test tubes)

(Lights off. All out)

SCENE 4

(The room is dimly lit. Nira lies on the bed, the vial of the Shetty's vaccine on the bedside table, glinting mysteriously. She takes a deep breath, her face a canvas of contemplation and uncertainty)

NIRA: (murmuring to herself) This vial, this tiny thing, could change everything. But it's so new, so uncharted.

GRANDFATHER:(leaning on the door frame)It's more than just the solution, Nira. It's the future of DeltaMedix Pharmaceuticals. It's the countless nights of hard work, the countless dreams.

NIRA: But Grandpa, it's also a gamble. A leap into the unknown. If this goes wrong, VedicPharm will be miles ahead.

AUNT RADHA: (walking over to sit next to her)Yes, the stakes are high. We're on the verge of either a breakthrough or a breakdown. But isn't that the point of innovation?

NIRA:(her voice trembling)The world is watching. Waiting. Every second counts, and here I am, paralyzed by fear.

COUSIN VEDANT: (joining them) We've always been pioneers, Nira. We've always taken risks. This isn't any different.

NIRA: But it is, Vedant. This isn't just about profit or the company's reputation. It's about people's lives.

GRANDFATHER: (with a sigh) The most significant changes are sometimes the result of the greatest risks. We must have faith in the research, our staff's dedication, and our mission.

NIRA: (tears forming) I want to, Grandpa. But what if I'm the reason it all falls apart?

AUNT RADHA: (holding Nira's hand)Every step we've taken, every decision, has led us here. We trust you, and we believe in this. Remember, you're not alone in this.

NIRA: (taking a deep breath) This could change everything. For the sick, for the world, for us.

VEDANT: We've always been at the forefront, Nira. This is our moment.

GRANDFATHER: Your grandmother used to say, "In moments of doubt, listen to your heart." What does it tell you?

NIRA:(closing her eyes for a moment) That I need to try. For all those suffering. For us.

(With that, Nira carefully administers the vaccine. Minutes feel like hours as the room fills with palpable tension.)

NIRA:(voice quivering) I... I don't feel right. Something's... something's happening.

GRANDFATHER: (panic evident)Nira, talk to us. Stay with us!

AUNT RADHA: (trying to hold back tears) Stay strong, Nira. You're our beacon of hope. You have always been.

NIRA:(*gasping*)I need... Aarav... he should know...

(Nira sends a message with trembling hands: "Aarav, I took the vaccine. Something isn't quite right. The future of DeltaMedix Pharmaceuticals...")

VEDANT: (holding Nira's hand) Fight it, Nira. You've always been a fighter.

NIRA: (with her last bit of strength) I hope... I hope it's worth it. For everyone.

(The weight of the moment hangs heavy in the room as her eyes flutter and her grip loosens. The future, now more uncertain than ever, looms large. Everyone rushes to different corners, hoping to do something, but everything turns out even worse. The doctor is summoned; he examines her and informs them that there is little they can do other than let her rest.)

(All lights dim)

SCENE 5

(The room has an overwhelming atmosphere of melancholy. The silence broken by the soft beeping of medical machines. In the shadowed corners, Aarav stealthily moves, avoiding any gaze that might recognize him. He enters her room and finds her laying down. One could clearly tell how weak she looked and how badly she was suffering)

AARAV: (voice filled with anguish)Nira?

NIRA: (weakly, with a hint of surprise) Aarav? How...?

AARAV:(choking up)I had to see you. I couldn't stay away.

NIRA: (smiling faintly)I dreamed of this moment, of seeing you again.

AARAV: (holding back tears) And I, of a world where you weren't confined to this room.

NIRA: (touching his hand) Our love story, though brief, feels endless.(tears) And in this eternity, I discovered a lifetime of love with you.

AARAV: Nira, I wish I could take away your pain, rewrite our story. Trust me, I'm almost done with the vaccine. I just want to try it if it's safe. Just some more tests and it will be done, I promise. Please stay until then. Please don't give up on yourself and us.

NIRA: (smiling through her tears) Some stories are written in the stars and cannot be changed. Nonetheless, they shine brightly

AARAV:(leaning closer) I'd trade all my tomorrows for one more today with you.

NIRA: (her voice is fading) Promise me something, Aarav.

AARAV: Anything, my love.

NIRA: (whispering in Aarav's ear) Promise me that no one else will suffer this way. Find that solution, that vaccine. Let our love be the catalyst for a world free from this pain.

AARAV: (tears streaming)I promise, Nira. Your wish, our dream, will be my life's mission.

NIRA: (her energy waning)Hold me, just once more.

(Aarav embraces Nira, holding her close. As moments pass, her breathing becomes shallower, her grip loosens)

AARAV: (voice breaking) Nira? NIRA!

NIRA: (her voice barely a whisper)I love you, Aarav.

(Nira's eyes flutter and she closes her eyes on the comfort of Aarav's lap. She becomes cold)

AARAV:(tears flowing freely)I love you too, Nira. I love you more than anything in this world.

(As a testament to a love that has defied the odds, Aarav places a gentle, heartfelt kiss on her forehead)

(The silence returns to the room, more profound than before, leaving Aarav holding an unconscious Nira, tears cascading down his face. The weight of love, loss, and a promise hanging heavy in the air.)

(Lights dim. Exeunt)